Secret of the Djinn

Jean Rabe

SECRET OF THE DJINN

All characters in this book are fictitious. Any resemblance to actual persons, living or dead, is purely coincidental.

This book is protected under the copyright laws of the United States of America. Any reproduction or other unauthorized use of the material or artwork herein is prohibited without the express written permission of TSR, Inc.

Random House and its affiliate companies have worldwide distribution rights in the book trade for English language products of TSR, Inc.

Distributed to the book and hobby trade in the United Kingdom by TSR Ltd.

Distributed to the toy and hobby trade by regional distributors.

Cover art by Jeff Easley.

Interior art by Terry Dykstra.

ENDLESS QUEST is a registered trademark owned by TSR, Inc. AL-QADIM and the TSR logo are trademarks owned by TSR, Inc.

First Printing: May 1994
Printed in the United States of America
LIBRARY OF CONGRESS CATALOG CARD NUMBER: 94-60099

9 8 7 6 5 4 3 2 1

ISBN: 1-56076-864-9

TSR, Inc.	TSR Ltd.
P.O. Box 756	120 Church End, Cherry Hinton
Lake Geneva, WI 53147	Cambridge CB1 3LB
United States of America	United Kingdom

PROLOGUE

n this book you are Jamil, a young pearl diver from Zakhara, a fabled realm much like the one described in tales such as "Ali Baba and the Forty Thieves" and "Aladdin and His Magic Lamp."

You live in Jumlat, one of Zakhara's busiest coastal cities. Like many of the residents there, you struggle hard to make your way in this world. You earn a living harvesting pearls from the Golden Gulf.

Your clothes are worn and faded, your purse contains but a few coins, and your only weapon is an old curved dagger. Still, you dream of rising above this meager existence to become one of the wealthy and important people of Zakhara.

Zakhara, also called the Land of Fate, is a place filled with powerful djinn, flying carpets, and untold wealth. It is a magical land of beauty and wonder! But it is also a land of challenges and danger, of loyal friends and menacing foes.

You know you must overcome the perils of this kingdom to gain fame and fortune and to make your dreams come true.

The adventure before you reads like a book. As you progress through the story, you will be offered choices. These choices are clearly indicated, and the path you take will determine your fate. Simply put, you will determine how the story ends.

Good luck, Jamil. The Land of Fate awaits you.

Go right on to 1.

1

"Jamil!" The cry cuts through the gray sky and stirs you from a sound slumber. "Jamil! Wake up! If we're late again, we'll have to beg for a living. Hurry!"

You yawn and toss back the covers. Scrambling to the window, you peer down from your second-story room and see your friend Ubar waving frantically. He stands amidst the shadow-draped stalls of Jumlat's marketplace. The marketplace is silent now, but it will be teeming with life in several hours. The wonderful hustle and bustle of the marketplace is not for you and Ubar, however.

Not today, at least.

You wipe the sleep from your eyes. It is nearly dawn. Though most of the citizens of Jumlat, City of Multitudes, still dream on, it is time for you to begin a long day's work.

"Jamil! Let's get going! Essaf will have our hides if the boat has to wait for us."

You nod to Ubar, dress quickly, and grab your curved dagger. Dashing downstairs, you join your friend, and the two of you dart between the silent marketplace stalls toward the docks.

"Jamil, you'll sleep your life away if you're not careful!" Ubar scolds. "What would you do if I wasn't here to wake you?"

"I would get more rest," you answer and pick up the pace. Ubar is eighteen, only one year older than you are, but often he acts like an old man, always worrying about something. You, on the other hand, seldom worry about anything.

"Maybe we'll dive near the monster today," Ubar pants without breaking stride. He notes your puzzled expression and explains. "Just south of here, near Gana, fishermen are disappearing. A sea monster the size of a great ship is eating them, the dockhands say. There's certain to be a reward for killing the beast."

You reach the harbor with Ubar at your heels. He is

still chattering about the creature, which is now the size of ten ships. You are just in time to see the first rays of the sun inching across the Golden Gulf's mirrorlike inner bay.

Already several other divers are on the docks. They sit with the oysters they gathered yesterday, cracking them open and removing the pearls. They set aside the meat, which will be sold in the marketplace. Nothing taken from the Golden Gulf is wasted.

You join the other divers, who mumble about your lateness. Shrugging off their remarks, you begin cracking open your oysters. Ubar works at your side. In less than an hour, your task is finished.

"I am fortunate!" you brag, displaying the handful of pearls your oysters yielded.

The other divers frown, and you grin broadly at them. You don't let them see that you are a little disappointed. Your oysters gave up only white pearls. You had hoped to find some of the prized pink-tinted ones that match the color of the early evening sky. You have found only a few pink pearls in the two years you have been diving. You have yet to capture any of the rare black ones that are sought everywhere up and down the coast of Zakhara. Such pearls net handsome bonuses for the divers.

Essaf the Hungry, the silk-draped captain of the boat on which you work, watches intently to make sure no pearls find their way into the divers' pockets. Essaf is a lean man who is ravenous only for wealth. It is he who prospers from an abundant harvest of pearls, not the men who dive. You and the other divers are paid only a fraction of what the pearls are worth.

Would that you could dive on your own. But for that you would need your own boat and your own rope boy. At the moment, you haven't nearly enough coins for either.

The breeze picks up, playing gently across your skin. With it comes the faint, salty smell of the sea. It is early spring, the beginning of the pearl-diving season. For the next five months, you and the others will work for Essaf, diving during the cool early morning and into and beyond the brutal heat of midday.

You will earn enough to pay for food, lodging, and clothes for the rest of the year. Then you will return the following spring to start diving all over again.

Someday you will no longer have to do this, you vow, cracking open the last of your oysters. Fate will smile upon you, and you will be richer than the Hungry One.

Someday you will have your own boat—no, a hundred boats. Each will have fifty divers and as many rope boys. Each practiced crew will harvest a fortune for you during pearl season. You will be a caliph before ten more years pass! You will have the most beautiful harem girls in all of Zakhara. You will have a quartet of the prettiest and cleverest wives.

You will be respected. You will be honored. You will never work for anyone again.

"Jamil! Snap to it!" Essaf bellows, rousing you from your pleasant musings. "Time to go! Move along or I'll demote you to rope boy."

Rope boy! Hah! You know Essaf wouldn't demote

you. You are his best diver, even though you are his youngest. You can stay at the bottom for nearly three minutes at a time. You are a strong swimmer, and you make dozens of dives each day. Still, you jump to your feet, bow to Essaf, and grudgingly follow the other divers onto the boat.

The boat eases almost silently away from the dock. The only sounds are the soft splashing of the oars as they slice through water tinged gold by the rising sun. Soon the breeze catches the sails, and the vessel picks up speed. The rowers abandon the oars to tend to other work while you and the rest of the divers prepare your equipment and check the ropes. You note that today the boat travels farther out than usual, into waters unfamiliar to you.

"A deep dive today," the Hungry One explains as he rolls a milky white pearl around between his thumb and middle finger. He paces back and forth on the crowded deck and nods to each diver. "You will dive at a depth of about seventy feet. These are good waters for oysters. Bring me pearls . . . hundreds of oysters filled with fat, pink pearls."

You undress and don a linen loincloth. All the divers wear loincloths and soft leather gloves to keep their fingers from getting cut by the oyster shells. Over your neck you place a net bag, which you intend to stuff with pearl-filled oysters, and you clench your dagger between your teeth. The blade comes in handy from time to time when oysters are stuck to rocks.

Hanging from the outside of the boat are thick hemp ropes with stones tied to their ends. You grab the side of the boat, step on a stone, take a deep breath, and nod to your rope boy. As he lowers the rope, the stone serves as an anchor, and its weight propels you quickly to the bottom of the Golden Gulf.

Down.
Down.
Down.

Finally reaching the bottom, you tug on the hemp rope about your diving stone, and the boy far above begins to pull it to the surface. Essaf wasn't joking when he said you would dive seventy feet. You are at least that far below the waves this morning. You swim south from the boat. Your course takes you only a foot or so above the sand, and you begin to look for oysters that are likely to hold pearls. Nearby, you see other divers searching the bottom. A dozen dive at a time. You vow today to bring in the most oysters and to make the most dives.

You are used to shallower waters, where the sun cuts more easily through the waves and lights the bottom. Here the water appears murky, though clean, and it is more difficult to spot the oysters hidden among the rocks and large shells. Still, you don't give up easily. If the Hungry One wants pink pearls, you will get them for him.

There! you think as you spot a cluster of oysters. Swimming quickly toward it, you tug the oysters free and gather them in your net bag.

That should be enough for the first trip!

Glancing up at the hull of Essaf's ship, you pump hard with your legs and shoot toward the surface. As you rise, you notice you stayed down longer than the other divers. Pride swells your chest. You have pledged to be the best diver in Jumlat, and you are pushing yourself to make your claim come true.

It seems as if it takes an eternity to reach the surface. Your lungs scream for air. You squint upward, judging how many feet you have to go. Then you glance toward the bottom, glimpsing in the distance a dark shape that you did not notice while you hugged the sand.

Partially hidden by rocks and sea fronds, it could be a sea creature. The monster rumored to be terrorizing fishermen near Gana? Surely Ubar's tale is true and a great reward awaits the diver who kills the beast!

Your head breaks clear of the water, and you breathe in great gulps of air. Though you stayed down too long, you will not admit this to the other divers or to the rope boys. Climbing onto the deck of the boat, you pour the oysters into your box and motion to your rope boy that you want to go back down right away. Surprised, he helps you mount the diving rock.

A deep breath and a moment later you are on the gulf floor again, headed toward the dark shape. Fortunately the other divers haven't noticed it yet. You would hate to share the reward.

You see a soft yellow glow coming from what must be the creature's head. The glow, large and unblinking, must be the sea monster's eyes.

You swim closer . . . closer.

You hold your knife firmly in your right hand, ready to stab at the creature with the sharp blade.

You will be rich.

The beast makes no move as you approach. After a few strokes forward, your hopes are dashed as you see the reason for its inactivity. It is a ship, not a creature! Disappointed, you note that the rotted hull of the vessel is buried in the sand. This ship probably sank several decades ago. But something inside is shining through a porthole, something that made you think the ship was a beast with glowing eyes.

You realize you should forget about the ship and go back to gathering oysters. There could be nothing of value left inside, could there? Surely whatever it carried was retrieved by divers decades ago.

Even so, you find yourself looking at its decaying timbers, thinking about riches, and swimming closer still. Perhaps there are oysters clustered at the base of the hull—oysters filled with pink and black pearls. Or perhaps a magical lantern is causing the yellow glow. Such a wondrous item would be worth much in the marketplace.

Your churning arms propel you forward. Colorful queen angelfish dart out of your path, and crabs skitter away from the hull. Finding a hole in the side of the sunken wreck, you pull yourself inside.

It is dark in here.

Very dark.

The early morning sun above does little but create thick, gray shadows. Your chest begins to hurt, and you find no sign of what is causing the yellow light.

You need air. Your head begins to pound, and you feel your heart beat. If you don't swim for the surface quickly, you'll drown in this wreck.

You are almost ready to turn back and swim for the Hungry One's boat when you spot the pale glow again. It is coming from a glass bottle deeper inside the wreck. The bottle's light dances and flickers, beckoning you near. Like a marionette being pulled by an invisible string, you close the distance to the bottle and try to ignore the throbbing pulses in your head and chest.

Your hands shakily lock about the fluted glass neck, and you hear a soft yet sultry voice inside your head.

Free me, O Prince. Free me.

Startled, your mouth gapes open, and you swallow a gulp of cold salt water. Is your air-starved brain making you hear things? You realize you are light-headed, and you sputter to force out the salt water.

Free me, O Prince. Free me, the voice persists.

Your chest burns for air, and for a moment you almost lose your grip on the glowing flagon.

Free me, the voice repeats insistently.

Perhaps on their own, perhaps guided by Fate, your fingers wrench loose the sodden cork. A blinding light engulfs the water around you.

The light is so intense you close your eyes and gasp in surprise. This is it, you realize. You will die here. You will drown, and your body will join whatever bones lie within this rotting hull. You gasp once more, and your lungs fill with sweet air.

Air?

"My Prince! I owe you my life!"

You take the air deep into your aching lungs and slowly open your eyes. The glow has softened and turned orange, like a Zakharan summer sunset. Though water remains all about you, there is a bubble of air around your head.

Sitting on an old sea chest where the glowing bottle once rested is the most beautiful woman you have ever seen. Your eyes pop wide in surprise, and you waggle

your fingers in front of your face to make sure you are conscious, not suffering some delusion as you die beneath the waves. No, you are not dying.

She smiles at you.

Her deep-green form is clothed in a short, silky white tunic edged in pearls, and her waist-length hair, the color of sea foam, twirls like seaweed caught in a gentle current. Her emerald eyes sparkle mischievously.

"My Prince. I am most humbly grateful to you. Do you have a name, my champion?"

You are so entranced by her beauty that it takes you several moments to reply. "J-J-Jamil," you finally stutter. "I am Jamil, a pearl diver." A grin spreads wide across your face. The most beautiful woman in all of the Land of Fate is grateful to you—*indebted* to you. Despite her green skin, you know that when she walks through the marketplace at your side she will be the envy of every woman and the desire of every man.

"You are more than a pearl diver, Jamil. You are my champion," the green woman purrs.

Her words are sweeter than ripe sugar apples, and your mind drifts away from the pearling boat and Essaf far above.

The water shimmers about the green woman, and the orange glow intensifies. She begins to grow. Eight feet. Ten feet. Fifteen feet. She bursts through the rotted deck of the ship and takes you and your air bubble with her. She is nearly twenty feet tall!

Your mind reels, and you flail about with your arms until you find a beam of wood to grasp on to. You lock your elbows about the wood, anchoring yourself, then risk a glance at her.

You see her looking westward. Following her gaze, you spy the frightened forms of your fellow pearl divers swimming frantically toward Essaf's boat above. You see Ubar, who escapes with them, terrified of the giant green woman.

"Wh-Wh-Wh-What are you?" you stammer.

"I am Tala, a marid—a djinni of the seas," she replies. "I am one of the most powerful of my kind,

and I am the queen of the Citadel of Ten Thousand
Pearls."

"Citadel of Pearls?"

She laughs, and sea fronds dance merrily about her.
"Mortal, the Citadel of Ten Thousand Pearls is the secret
home of all the sea djinn. It is a wondrous place like no
other in the Land of Fate." Tala gestures with her hand,
and you and your air bubble spin toward her.

"For all my power, I was helpless. You saved me,
Jamil. And now you must save my husband, the king,
so we can return to the Citadel and take our places
upon the pearl thrones."

"Husband?" You stare at her with a puzzled expression. Your dream of walking with her through the Jumlat marketplace suddenly fades.

"For sixty years I have not seen he who is my beloved.
It was sixty years ago that an ancient sha'ir, a truly
malicious wizard, tricked my husband and me," the
beautiful marid begins. "We had befriended the old
wizard. But he was crafty for a human, and he betrayed
us. He used his spells to capture us and our considerable treasure. The twisted man magically imprisoned
us in bottles before we could act, and he spirited away
all our gold and pearls. My bottle he placed in this
wreck. My husband's bottle he kept in his tower."

"Listen," you say softly, "I rescued you by accident. I
was looking for pearls. I couldn't save your husband,
even if I knew where he was. I'm a pearl diver. I'm not a
hero."

The sea djinni furrows her brow, and in response the
sea grows dark and still around her. Fish dart away
quickly, and you tremble in fear.

"The sha'ir's tower is in Sikak, City of Coins," Tala
announces flatly. "I will summon a strong wind to fly
us there so you can rescue my beloved who is the king
of the Citadel of Ten Thousand Pearls."

"Fly? You're not listening to me."

"You must free my husband because the sha'ir has
spells that allow him to trap djinn," she persists. "To
trap djinn even as powerful as I. I do not wish to be

enslaved again. A human . . . a simple human pearl diver . . . might be beneath his notice."

"I told you, I'm not a hero." Your mind whirls. Sixty years ago the *old* sha'ir trapped them. He has to be dead by now, you think. It might even be impossible to find the bottle after all these decades.

You glance at the marid. Her eyes flash like sparkling gems as she returns your stare.

"What say you, Jamil? Will you rescue my husband, the king of the Citadel of Ten Thousand Pearls? Or will you return to your life of diving for pearls—pearls that will line your taskmaster's pockets?"

If you agree to aid the sea djinni, turn to 5.
If you tell the djinni she should find another person to help her, turn to 8.

2

The djinni floats above you, expecting an answer to her question.

"My sister!" you blurt out. "I've come to rescue my sister. She's in Sha'ir Rashad's harem. My poor, sick mother is worried about her. We need my sister home to take care of my mother so she can get well."

The djinni's eyebrows raise, and she floats closer.

"Your sister. She is young?"

"Yes. Too young, my mother says, to be away from home." You smile thinly for effect, pleased that your lie sounds so convincing. "The sha'ir will not miss one harem girl. And my mother needs her daughter by her side. Please don't stop me."

The djinni smiles slowly. "No. My master Rashad al-Azzazi would not miss one harem girl. He has been so busy lately he has paid no attention to them at all. Tell me your sister's name and what she looks like. I will retrieve her for you."

You stammer. "Her name. Um. Her name is Farida. She looks a lot like me, but she's pretty."

The djinni chortles. "Farida? The name is unfamiliar to me, and I know the names of all those who work and walk within the rose tower. And I don't recall seeing any harem girl that looks remotely like you, *but pretty*. I think, Jamil, that you are lying. And I think my master Rashad al-Azzazi would like to find out the truth."

Turn to 22.

3

The carpet carries you far from the island of giant trees and out over the sea. It is night, and there are plenty of stars to keep you company. Judging by the constellations, you can tell the carpet is taking you northeast.

You now have two pieces of the carpet. The tan djinni who serves Sha'ir Rashad al-Azzazi told you there are four. When placed together, they create a map that will lead to a dead man's treasure trove. And, hopefully, inside the treasure trove will be a bottle with a fluted neck—and inside the bottle the king of the Citadel of Ten Thousand Pearls.

You drift off to sleep, dreaming of treasure and the beautiful green djinni you rescued from the bottom of the Golden Gulf.

You awaken at sunrise. A soft rain is falling on you. It feels good against your skin. The drops plink upon the blade of your scimitar and make it glisten in the light of the early day.

Where are we going? you wonder as you peer over the edge of the carpet. Below lies a mountain range, though what mountain range, you couldn't begin to guess. You never cared much for studies, not even about your own country, but now you wish you had paid a little more attention to geography.

The carpet suddenly dips and dives toward the bleakest-looking mountain. Your stomach protests the plunging sensation, and you close your eyes so you won't get sick. You spiral quickly downward, and you hold on to your scimitar with one hand and the carpet with the other. If you were to fall off now, the green djinni would have to scrape you off the rocks and find another champion.

Finally the carpet comes to rest on a rocky outcrop on the mountainside. The rug does little to protect your bottom from the jagged stone beneath it. You rub your sore behind and glance up and down the mountain. The next piece of carpet is nowhere to be seen.

"Wonderful," you say to yourself. "I'll bet it's near the top. Fate would not be so kind as to make my path easy." That said, you roll up both pieces of carpet, stick them under your arm, and start a long climb up the side of the mountain.

The hours pass, and you feel like you've walked forever. Looking up, you study the sun, which persistently bakes your arms, torso, and face. It's only noon. You wonder where Essaf the Hungry and his pearl divers are. Probably near water where it is cool, you decide. Ah, for just a few swallows of water.

"Ouch!" you cry, as the sharp rocks of the mountainside dig into your feet. Pearl divers have little need for sandals, but would-be heroes definitely need something to keep their soles from bleeding. Gritting your teeth in an attempt to ignore the pain, you continue your climb. Higher, higher. Three hours later, the sun has made your skin uncomfortably hot, and you are halfway up the mountainside.

You get an odd feeling that someone is watching you. It's merely because you are tired, you tell yourself. But the feeling persists. Turning and glancing down the mountain, you spy a lone figure slowly climbing toward you—following the exact path you took. The figure is dressed from head to toe in black, and a hood shadows his face. A massive sword hangs at his side.

You turn to gaze at the top of the mountain, which is not much farther. If you can claim the third piece of the carpet, you can fly away and not worry whether the man in black is a friend or foe. You wipe the sweat from your face with your forearm and squint upward.

No! There is another figure, high on the mountain-side. Silhouetted against the blazing sun is the form of a turbaned man who clutches a gnarled staff. The figure is tall, though not of immense proportions. A hermit, perhaps, or crazy mountain-dweller. With measured, accustomed steps, he gravitates slowly toward you, pebbles dancing down the slope before him.

It looks like you will have company, Jamil. The question is, who should you meet first? It is obvious you cannot avoid both of them.

Do you stay where you are and let the turbaned man approach? If so, turn to 11.

Or, do you climb back down to encounter the man in black. If this is what you do, turn to 7.

4

You stare at the giant, magically suspended in time. If the spell that holds him ends, his club might come down upon your head. That is provided you stay in the same spot.

You roll out from under the hulking form and glance at the green djinni.

"I told you before, I don't want to help you," you state simply. "I'll stick with that decision."

"You are most foolish," Tala remarks in surprise. Her emerald eyes glare irately. "Very well, Jamil, the pearl diver—-Jamil, the fool. I will leave you to your fate, and I will travel the Crowded Sea until I can find a human champion who is worthy of rescuing the king of the Citadel of Ten Thousand Pearls."

The marid disappears in a puff of sea-green smoke that quickly dissipates in the branches.

"Yum!" erupts the one-eyed giant, held no longer by the djinni's magic. With great force he brings his club down upon the ground where you were moments before.

"Huh? Where little snack go?" The giant whirls, and you see his sole eye narrow in outrage. "Little snack tries to run away!" He shoulders his great club and swings it at your head. You deftly dodge and glance about, wondering where you should run.

"Little snack is dead!" the giant cries.

With great force he brings his club down upon you. This time you didn't dodge in time.

The world goes black.

THE END

5

The marid stares at you, her emerald eyes flashing. She wants an answer.

You have no desire to risk your life by angering a powerful sha'ir, you think to yourself. But it is more than likely the sha'ir is dead, and therefore can pose no threat. After all, he was old when he imprisoned her—and that was sixty years ago.

The marid is a more immediate threat. With a thought, she could burst this bubble of air that surrounds you and drown you, and perhaps drown all those on the ship, too, for good measure. Besides, she'll probably leave you alone if you can prove the old sha'ir died years ago.

Forcing a smile, you meet the djinni's emerald gaze. "I'll help you, Tala," you hear yourself say. In your heart you know there was no other answer to give her.

"You are wise beyond your years, Jamil the pearl diver." Tala stretches her hands above her head, and you and your air bubble are pulled upward. "Together we shall fly to Sikak. The workings of the evil sha'ir shall soon be undone. Come, my human champion."

The bubble collapses and you feel the cool water surround you. For an instant you fear that you will drown anyway, but Tala's large hand grabs you about the waist, and she rises magically from the sea bottom.

As her massive green head breaks the surface, you hear the gasps of the pearl divers and rope boys.

"Look! A sea djinni! It's got Jamil!" one of them cries. It is your friend Ubar who points toward you and the marid. "Captain Essaf, we must do something!"

The Hungry One looks on and steps behind a group of gaping rope boys for protection. "We can do nothing!" he bellows.

You smirk. You have more courage in one of your strands of hair than Essaf has in his entire body.

The marid closes her eyes, and an instant later her giant form disappears—to be replaced by one closer to your own size, still green.

You glance once again toward the boat. One of the divers points your way and shouts, but you can't hear what he is saying. However, you see Essaf the Hungry One looking on in amazement and perhaps fear. You wonder if he will give you a job again when your grand adventure is over.

"Ready, Jamil?" the soft voice purrs.

You nod, she grasps your hand, and you find yourself being lifted again, this time above the water. The green djinni flies with you in tow over the pearling boat, then climbs high into the sky.

You have begun your magical journey to Sikak, and you quiver from the cold as the air dries the water from your skin. You shiver from fear more than from the chill as the sensation of flying is new and terrifying. You pray to Haku that Tala's grip is strong, or you will join the fishes in the waters far, far below.

The sea looks like a painting from your bird's-eye view. It is still and beautiful, and the waves are tiny white flecks. Ahead and below you see the shores of Zakhara, the Land of Fate.

You fly over your home city of Jumlat, and the buildings look like doll houses, small and fragile and unreal. You squint to make out the antlike forms of people. And there is the marketplace. Colorful tents and awnings peek through the dollhouse buildings.

You pass over the city and continue north. You spy

the Al-Fatir, the Tepid River, snaking like a blue ribbon toward the desert and the Mountains of Tears beyond.

You begin to enjoy yourself. If Ubar and the other divers could see you now they would be filled with awe and envy. Oh, how you wish they could see you!

Tala breaks the silence. "Sixty years was I trapped in that bottle. Those years might have brought change to Sikak. What can you tell me of the City of Coins?"

"I have never been there," you state, noticing that your mouth and throat are dry from the wind. "But I know the ruler is a gnome, a little wrinkled man no taller than my waist. He is a most well-loved ruler, they say. I know there are many sha'irs and other wizards in the city. Sikak reeks of magic—or so the people of Jumlat and the other Pearl Cities claim."

Scanning the ground, you watch as the marid's path follows the coastline. The Bountiful Shoals, a fisherman's delight, lies ahead, its coral reefs making the water appear orange and yellow in places. Tala angles her course to the northwest, and the City of Coins is revealed in all its splendor.

Your mouth gapes open. From your skyward position, the city is beautiful, a jewel set against the Bountiful Shoals. Its spires and domes glitter in the sun. The city's marketplace is larger than Jumlat's, and the banners and awnings are colorful and inviting. Through a break in the buildings you spy the Al-Nuhas River, the River of Copper. Indeed, from this high up its waters glitter like coins. Perhaps this is how proud Sikak got its name.

"It will not be long now, Jamil," Tala whispers as she takes your path lower.

The ground rushes up to meet you, and Tala steers the two of you toward a small grove of trees just south of the city. There, she sets you down. The earth feels good beneath your feet, and you almost lose your balance on it as she releases your hand.

"Look, my champion!" the marid exclaims, pointing through the trees. "See the rose-colored tower? The one apart from all the other tall buildings?"

You nod, still entranced by the sights of the City of Coins.

"That is the sha'ir's tower. Sha'ir Rashad al-Azzazi, the human who dared to rob sixty years from my husband and me, the human who dared to confine our power." Her voice is sharp and bitter, and as she continues, you note that her skin becomes a darker green.

The marid turns her gaze to you, and her emerald eyes flash indignantly. "Well, what are you waiting for, Jamil? There is his tower. Now, go find my husband. Hurry, Jamil, I will wait for you here. If you are not back by nightfall, I will come search for you. But be warned, Jamil the pearl diver, I will not confront the sha'ir to save you. Even I fear his power, and I do not wish to be in a bottle for another six decades."

With that, you strike off toward the tower, pondering how to get inside the rose-colored building in Sikak, City of Coins.

Turn to 24.

6

Again you step into the darkened passageway, though this time you are not surprised when the blackness surrounds you. You take a few deep breaths to calm your jangled nerves, then stalk forward, walking your fingertips along the rough-hewn wall to guide your way. The floor of the passageway feels smooth against your bare feet, and as you inch forward, you can tell that it gets cooler.

The old sha'ir could not have constructed this place, you are convinced. Though he surely commanded much magic to capture two djinn, this place is centuries old and was shaped by the forces of nature and time. Perhaps the sha'ir accidently came upon it, falling through the sands like yourself. Or perhaps he learned of it from a storyteller in the marketplace.

No matter, you are certain that it has been a very,

very long time since someone journeyed down here, and you suspect it was hands other than the sha'ir's that painted the flying eagles.

How the sha'ir learned of this fortress is unimportant, you decide. What is important is that he knew a section of his carpet would be safe here.

You take another step forward and squint. Again light spills from your lantern. The blackness has ended, replaced by a shadow-swathed chamber coated with spider webs and dust—and filled with gold and beautiful treasures. As your eyes adjust to the dim light and the array of wealth, you attempt to take it all in.

"Haku be praised!" you gasp in awe. "I shall be rich!"

This must be the old sha'ir's treasure trove!

Mounds of gold dinars cover the chamber, piled like dirt about an anthill. Though coated with dust, the coins gleam dully in the lantern light. Intermingled with the gold are pools of silver coins and necklaces of silver, pearls, and ivory beads. Veritably a caliph's ransom is laid out before you! As you stoop to look at a few of the coins, more treasures catch your eye. There are loose gems here, as well, tucked between the gold and silver. Emeralds, rubies, sapphires, and jacinths. There! Over there is a topaz the size of your fist!

Brass lamps poke out of the mounds of coins, as do candle holders, ornate brooches circled with the finest of pink pearls, silk slippers, coral anklets, gem-studded scabbards, hammered gold girdles, jeweled agals, and more.

The hoard has been here a few decades at least, judging from the dust and spiderwebs. Surely its owner won't mind if you sample a bit of the treasure. You'll take just a few pieces—enough to make you unbelievably rich. The sha'ir cannot possibly notice a few pieces missing.

You stride forward, feeling the coins beneath your feet and not minding their uneven surface. There is so much treasure in this chamber that you can't avoid stepping on some of it.

"If only Essaf's rope boys could see this, could see me," you muse as your gaze continues to drink in all the wealth before you. "I could buy a fleet of pearling boats."

"Why would you want pearling boats in the desert?"

The booming voice fills the chamber and stops you in your tracks. A chill races up and down your spine as you slowly turn your head and take in the speaker.

A giant of a man moves from behind the largest mound of gold dinars. His head nearly touches the ceiling, and his shoulders are as broad as you are tall. He easily measures twenty feet tall.

You shiver and swallow hard.

"I said, why would you want boats in the desert?"

"I-I-I-I was just dreaming," you finally stammer. "I am from Jumlat, on the Golden Gulf. I work on a boat."

You watch his muscles ripple as he clenches and releases his fists and strides forward on hairy legs that end in hooves.

"You're a long way from the Golden Gulf, little one. Did you come here by camel? Or did a strong wind push your boat across the sand?"

"It's a long story," you start, "I guess you could say, indirectly, that a djinni of the sea brought me here."

"Hmmm. Djinni tricksters are known for sending people where they don't belong. It is too bad you ran afoul of one."

"You don't understand," you protest. "I want to be here. Well, I *guess* I want to be here. I'm looking for something."

"Looking for something for the sea djinn?"

"Well, yes. Something to rescue her husband."

The giant scowls, displaying a row of unusually perfect teeth. "It is an odd story. I do not believe you."

Frustrated, you glare at him. "I don't have to explain myself to you. I just need to gather a few things and be on my way."

The giant leans forward and scratches his smooth, hairless chin. "I can't let you do that."

"And why not?" You puff out your chest in an

attempt to bluff the creature.

"I guard this place, a minor treasure chamber of an old sha'ir. He would take exception to parting with any of his baubles and dinars."

"That sha'ir is dead."

"You have proof?"

You grind the ball of your foot into the coins. No. You don't have proof. You don't have the dead sha'ir's body to hold out. And you don't have his grandson to recount the tale of the old man's death. You opt to try another tack.

"Listen, no one would miss just a few bits of treasure. Let me have some, and I'll tell you a wondrous story. I'll bet you could use the company. Do you have some food to share? Some water?"

"It has been seven decades since the sha'ir visited with me," the giant stated simply. "I would enjoy your company. But you cannot take any of the treasure."

"You've been here all that time? Alone?" you ask incredulously. "What do you eat? What do you do? Why are you here? Can you leave?"

The giant smiles sadly. "I eat nothing. Somehow I am never hungry. Somehow I am never tired. I am never thirsty. And I will stay here until I die—if death is something that can claim me."

You stare at the creature more closely and note that its skin is not a natural color. The bronze of its flesh looks like true bronze, a metal, not tanned from the sun and the desert. At odd intervals are small bolts and seams.

"You are a construct!"

"I am a guardian."

"You're not even alive," you continue. "You're not breathing."

"I think. I count dinars. I talk to you. I am alive." The giant glares at you.

"Fine, you're alive."

"I am a guardian. You cannot have what I guard."

"Right." You pace back and forth, stepping on a bed of silver coins and nearly losing your footing.

Mustering your courage, you cross your arms in

front of your chest and glare up into his unlined face. "Fine. What if I just spend the night here? I'm tired. Then I'll be on my way." You pause and stare at him, trying to read some emotion in his metal features. "Is that a problem? Does the guardian need to guard the treasure from a sleeping man?"

For what seems an interminable amount of time, the guardian stands motionless, returning your gaze. Finally, it takes a step forward and waves its arm toward the center of the room. "Very well. Sleep here and I will guard you, too. When you are rested, you will go back the way you came—with none of the sha'ir's treasure in your pockets. You will get on your sand-bound boat and sail away from here."

Pushing aside silver and gold coins, you spread out your three sections of carpet and curl up on them between the mounds of treasure. The final piece of the carpet has to be here. Minor treasure chamber. Humph! You wonder what the treasure trove looks like where the king of the Citadel of Ten Thousand Pearls rests.

Feigning sleep will give you time to think. Maybe the giant will wander off and you can search for the carpet. You close your eyes and find yourself nearly drifting off. Indeed, the ordeals of this day have been taxing, and you are very tired. Perhaps it would not be so bad to take a little nap. Perhaps you could think much better if you rested. You relax and let your mind wander, drifting off to a welcomed sleep.

You awake hours later, shivering from the cold. You nudge open an eye. The giant construct is still there, watching you.

He is several feet away from you, and if you move swiftly, you could grab a few bits of treasure and flee. That would not net you the next piece of the carpet, however, which is probably lying somewhere beneath the coins. Still, it would gain you enough wealth to take a few years off work—provided you could find your way back home.

Or, you could lie here and think awhile longer. Perhaps you can come up with a better plan. Well, Jamil, what course of action will you take? Jump to your feet and grab a few choice bits of treasure? You are undoubtedly faster than this giant. Why, if you get enough wealth you can hire a group of nomads to come here and keep the construct occupied while you look for the piece of carpet. If you have enough nomads with you, the giant will fall before your numbers, and this treasure will be yours to divide.

If you decide to grab a little wealth and sprint from this chamber, turn to 44.

If, instead, you try to think of a better idea, turn to 47.

7

You decide to avoid the figure descending toward you and instead face the man in black, and you pick your way toward him. Perhaps he is familiar with these mountains and will help you find the third piece of the carpet. You slide your magic sword into a rolled up section of carpet and stick it under your arm. No use making him think you are hostile.

He waves a greeting as you approach, and you return the friendly gesture. But as you near him, something tugs at the corner of your mind. There is something familiar about him.

No! your mind shouts, look at his face! It is beardless, but those eyes are distinctive. It is the young Sha'ir Rashad al-Azzazi!

You turn around and scramble back up the side of the mountain. How could he have found you? Magic, no doubt. Magic or by coercing the tan djinni in his tower. Farther up the mountain is the turbaned man. Perhaps he can help you.

What to do? What to do?

You could face the sha'ir. Perhaps he can be reasoned with. No, you know better than that. But perhaps you could defeat him.

Or you could run toward the turbaned man. You certainly can't avoid both of them, and there is no place to hide on this rocky slope.

If you face the sha'ir, turn to 29.
If you seek refuge with the turbaned man, turn to 11.

8

You gape at the beautiful marid. "I'm sorry," you state simply. "I'm just a pearl diver. I told you I'm not a hero. You have to find someone else to help you rescue your husband."

"You refuse?!" Tala shrieks, her hair whipping about her head like a nest of mad sea snakes. She reaches out an emerald hand and grabs you roughly about the waist, knocking the wind from your lungs. "How dare you refuse the queen of the Citadel of Ten Thousand Pearls!"

She seems to grow even taller, and the air bubble about you shrinks. She gestures, and you see the water above you part, as if a great pair of hands were pulling it in two directions.

Looking up in horror, you see Essaf's ship hang suspended in the air for a moment, then plummet like a diving stone to the now-dry floor of the Golden Gulf's bay. The crash is deafening, and the screams of your friends maddening. The boat's timbers splinter like a child's toy against the rocks and hard sand of the sea floor.

You see the pearl divers and rope boys who survived the fall struggle to their feet. Around them lie the broken bodies of men who were not as fortunate. Ubar cradles a broken arm and stares at you—and at the giant marid who continues to bellow.

"Jamil!" she shouts, holding you in midair near her giant-sized face. "I will find another champion. One who is alive!"

The angry marid tosses you toward the ship and motions once more. You hear Ubar scream, a horrid gurgle that is drowned out by the sea. No longer held at bay by the marid's invisible force, the waves come crashing down on you and the pearling boat. As you plummet into the waters, you glimpse Ubar's form washing away from you, then the waves hammer you, the divers, and the rope boys.

Will drowning be painful? you wonder as the sea-water fills your lungs and another great, pounding wave beats you into merciful unconsciousness.

Time passes. Hours? Days?

You wake to the cries of gulls and find yourself sprawled on a floating piece of wood that is little bigger than yourself. Rubbing your fingers over its rough, painted surface, you realize it is part of Essaf's boat.

"How long?" you ask. How long have you been unconscious? You squint across the waves and rub your eyes with a sunburned hand. Days, you decide. Judging by the dryness of your skin, your parched throat, your rumbling belly, and your cracked lips, you have been asleep for a few days.

You are adrift—somewhere. You see no sign of the other pearl divers, the rope boys, or the Hungry One. You wonder if any of them are alive or if they paid the ultimate price for your refusal to help the beautiful marid.

Though you had never met a djinni before, you had heard tales of their power. It was foolish to anger her, you understand now. It would have been better for you, Ubar, and the other divers if you had tried to find her husband. In the back of your mind you hear their screams as the boat was demolished by the djinni as easily as a diver cracks open an oyster.

Trying to force away the haunting memories, you take in your watery surroundings. You gaze to the horizon.

Nothing.

No sign of land.

You are hungry and thirsty. You still have your curved dagger, but unless a fish swims very close to the surface, and is very slow and stupid, the blade will not help you net a meal.

You drift for hours, fading in and out of consciousness. In your waking moments you curse yourself for challenging a djinni. Finally, you spot . . . a sail?

There! You see a flicker of white. It is a sail! And beyond it, at the edge of your vision, you spot land! Praise to Haku! You will survive after all.

The choice is yours. Do you swim toward the ship? Or do you paddle toward the island? The land is farther away, but the boat is moving. And from your vantage point you cannot tell which direction the sails are taking it.

If you paddle toward the ship, head for 13.
If you make for the island, turn to 23.

9

The djinni floats above you, expecting an answer to her question.

"I don't want the sha'ir's treasure," you falter, opting for the truth. "I just want a bottle. It's an old bottle."

The djinni's expression reveals her curiosity. Floating to the landing, she steps toward you and scratches her head. "A bottle? You can easily buy bottles, even old ones, in the marketplace."

You sigh and begin your tale. "About sixty years ago the sha'ir captured a pair of marids, djinn of the sea, and hid them away in identical bottles. I accidently rescued one of them—a woman—when I was diving for pearls. She thinks her husband is imprisoned in a bottle in this tower."

The djinni's brow creases, and she snakes out a finger to poke at your chest. "So you want a marid, not a bottle. You want a sea djinni so you can have wishes and pearls!"

"No, no!" You shake your head vehemently. "I tried to tell you I already have one of the marids. Or, rather, *she* has *me*. I have to help her find her husband. I don't even want to think what she'll do to me if I come back without him."

You shake your head in dismay and continue. "You see, together they rule this place they call the Citadel of Ten Thousand Pearls."

"The Citadel?" the tan djinni exclaims. "The Citadel is the secret home of the sea djinn!"

"Yes, that's what she told me. She says she's the queen and her trapped husband is the king."

The tan djinni lets out a long breath and glances up the stairs behind her.

"Your story is too strange to be a lie, even for a human," she whispers. "My master, Sha'ir Rashad al-Azzazi has many djinn for servants: djinn of the desert, like me, djinn of the earth, and djinn of fire. But there are no sea djinn here."

"I told you, he's in a bottle. He's not just out floating around!" you fume. "The bottle's been lying around somewhere for sixty years."

"Sixty years? But my master is only thirty years old."

"I don't understand," you grumble, slumping on the stairway. "Sha'ir Rashad al-Azzazi was a formidable old man sixty years ago."

"Formidable he is," the tan djinni answers. "But truly, he is only thirty years old." She strokes her chin in contemplation. "However, he did have a grandfather by the same name, my previous master. His grandfather was also a powerful sha'ir."

That's it! The man who imprisoned the sea djinn is dead after all. His grandson of the same name owns the tower now and doesn't seem to care in the least about the old, dusty bottle.

"So maybe the bottle is still here. Help me find it. Let's go to the young Rashad al-Azzazi and ask him if he knows where it is!"

The djinni's eyes widen. "Ask him for nothing. He is not a kind man. If he were to learn about the king of the sea djinn, he'd hunt for the bottle and keep the king for himself. I have a better idea. If the bottle belonged to the sha'ir's grandfather, it has to be in the old man's treasure trove."

"Great. Let's go to the treasure trove!"

"We'll have to find it first," she replies.

You frown.

"Don't worry," the tan djinni brightens. "There's bound to be a map to it. My former master kept plenty of maps."

"All right. Let's say we find this map and I go to this trove. Will your new master notice when I get there? Does he have magic to warn him if someone breaks in?"

The tan djinni chuckles. "He doesn't even know his grandfather's treasure trove exists. I only do what my new master commands. He never commanded me to tell him anything about his grandfather. Come along. We must find the map and be on our way."

Our way? Does this djinni think she's coming with me? Before you can argue, you find the world spinning, the muted browns of the stairway run together, then brighten and turn white and rose and yellow. When the motion stops you find yourself in an immense room with a large pool in the center and chiseled marble columns supporting the roof. Three women swim leisurely in the pool, and for a moment you fear you have been spirited to the sha'ir's harem. Only the owner is permitted inside a harem. All others risk death. The tan djinni waves her fingers, and the girls stop moving, like floating statues.

You stride quickly to keep up with the djinni as her silent feet carry her past the columns. The soft slapping sound of your bare feet on the cool marble is the only noise in the room.

"Somewhere here. Somewhere," the djinni murmurs to herself. "Ah, yes." Reaching a place on the wall, the djinni runs her sand-colored hands over the stones until one moves inward slightly. She pushes hard, a section of the wall swings inward, and she floats inside.

You briskly follow and find yourself in a small room filled with hundreds of scrolls and thick, musty-smelling leather-bound books. She begins thumbing through the tomes and rolled parchments, reading at a speed you believed impossible.

Several minutes and hundreds of pages later, the djinni slams shut a large red leather book and squeals.

"This will be such fun, Jamil! This will truly be an adventure," she gushes.

You groan inwardly. You don't want an adventure. You just want to find the king and go home. You stare as she floats to the top of a tall bookshelf, moves several tomes around, and retrieves a rug.

"Here!" the tan djinni exclaims. "This is the first part of the map that leads to the treasure trove."

"First part?" This doesn't sound good, you think.

"Yes. My former master, the elder Rashad al-Azzazi, made his treasure map out of a large, wondrous carpet. According to his journal, he tore the carpet into four pieces and scattered them."

"Great. So we know how to get one-fourth of the way there." You slump dejectedly against the wall and wonder what the marid will say when you tell her this news.

"Don't be silly," the tan djinni scolds. "This is a magic carpet, a flying carpet. Just sit on it, and it will lead you to the other pieces! Put the pieces together and follow the golden threads to the treasure. Simple."

You shake your head numbly. "Nothing has been simple since I freed the marid."

She drops the section of the carpet to the floor and waves her arm, indicating that you should sit on the magical rug. You take a step forward to do just that when a shadow falls in your path.

"What treachery is this?" a voice booms. At the entrance to the secret room, a tall man with a braided black beard blocks the way. He is draped in a brocaded robe dotted with jewels; the garment must be worth the price of a large pearling ship, you think. On his head is a linen turban with an emerald clasp as big as your fist. His fingers are adorned up to the knuckles with gold and silver rings. His eyes are neither blue nor black, but some whirling combination of the two colors. They are active, lively eyes that take everything in and glare angrily at you and the djinni.

"Master Rashad al-Azzazi!" the djinni cries and falls to her knees.

"What are you doing, slave? And what is this room I knew nothing about?"

"It was your grandfather's room," she wails. "Do not punish me, master."

He glowers at the djinni, then turns his attention to you. You ease yourself to the side, so that you are standing on the carpet.

"I won't punish you much, slave, if you tell me what all of this is about. And who is he?" the sha'ir points a ring-encrusted finger at you. "Tell me everything djinni!"

"Flee, Jamil!" the djinni cries. "I must obey him! I will tell him everything! Flee while you can!"

Turn to 28.

10

Your curiosity could kill you, Jamil. Still, you find yourself padding toward the bowl-shaped depression where the giant roc landed. Imagine a bird big enough to carry an elephant in one claw! Perhaps the final piece of carpet you seek lies where the creature landed. Besides, that may indeed be a pool of water and not a mirage. You are thirsty, after all.

Praying to Haku of the Desert Winds that the roc does not see you, you run forward across the sand for nearly half a mile before you come to the bowl-shaped area in the desert that is the great bird's nest. There is no water next to it. Another mirage to dash your hopes.

Still, you are here; you might as well take a look at the great bird. You remember hearing stories that the giant rocs only came to roost on mountains, where they could survey all before them and swoop down upon the choicest of prey. If that is true, it would be odd for such a creature to roost in the desert. Of course, you suspect those who have survived an encounter with the great birds are few, and their information incomplete. This bird has chosen the flat expanse of desert for a nest, and perhaps there are no survivors to report the location of its home.

Dropping to your stomach in hopes the bird will not see you, you crawl forward over the sands until you are at the edge of the depression. You hold your breath, fearing the bird will spot you or hear you. And you peer into the basin, gritting your teeth in the hopes the elephant's death will not be too grisly to bear. . . .

You gasp in surprise. It is not the elephant that is being killed, but the roc. Though the bird is several times the size of the weathered-skinned pachyderm, it is being beaten beneath the trampling feet of its intended meal. Already the elephant has broken one of the giant roc's wings, and the bird flounders angrily in its nest, like a fly that has been swatted. The elephant's trumpeting grows louder in triumph as a wing snaps under the weight of its feet.

The great bird flounders about on its two legs, attempting to stay away from what it had once hoped would be its meal. But the elephant presses its attack, like a mouse assaulting a cat, darting in and out with amazing speed. Rearing back on its trunklike legs, the elephant brings its front feet crashing down on the great bird's neck. The roc's death spasms are sickening, and you turn your head to avoid witnessing the end.

Several moments later, you glance again into the depression to see the roc lying still and the elephant ambling up the sand toward you.

Haku, no! your mind screams. Is the elephant mad, and will it kill me next? Thoughts war within your head. There is nowhere to hide—the desert is so flat. Still, you will not make an easy victim for the vicious pachyderm. Scrambling to your feet, you begin to back away from the bowl just as the elephant's head clears the depression.

"Good afternoon, young man," the elephant says, a

bit out of breath. "I saw you watching the altercation."

You grunt in amazement that an elephant can talk and find yourself speechless for the moment.

"Ah, I see." The elephant stops and looks at you balefully. "You didn't think I would win." The creature makes a sound that is a cross between a sigh and a snort and shakes its massive head. You notice that the animal's sides are bloody, no doubt from where the roc dug its talons in.

"I knew I would win. I just had to wait until that disagreeable beast put me down. I was at quite a disadvantage in the air, you know. If I had killed the thing in the air, the roc would have dropped me. Even I couldn't have survived such a fall." The elephant grimaces and moves its trunk back and forth before extending it toward you, like a man would extend his hand in greeting. "I am Djuhah, the youngest—and most impetuous—son of Hatim al-Nisr, Caliph of Dakan. Wizard superb at one time, I could command the elements."

"You don't look like a caliph's son or a wizard," you finally muster, realizing if the animal were going to harm you, it would have done so by now.

"Ah, at one time I was both, and quite handsome— for a human," the elephant continues. "I still am handsome—for a pachyderm, that is. But, alas, my wizardly skills have all but vanished with my human form. You see, I chose to cherish the wrong woman. I fell deeply in love with a beautiful girl. She smelled of jasmine and had hair the color of onyx and eyes the color of sapphires. She happened to be the daughter of a powerful sha'ir in L'tiraf, City of Confessions."

The elephant stamps the ground with its right foot. Tears well up in the animal's eyes. "The sha'ir wanted her to marry someone else—a prince from Burj. I protested, and the sha'ir, who surprisingly possessed more magical prowess than I, called upon his pet djinni to turn me into this beast and spirit me far, far away. I wandered a bit too far out of the woods this morning, and that bird grabbed me. I'll be more careful in the future."

You grin and explain your own problems with djinn and the sha'ir from Sikak, and the two of you while away the next hour discussing how much better Zakhara would be without evil wizards and djinn. Finally, the elephant bids you farewell, saying he plans to return to the Sheltered River.

"I have accepted my lot in life, Jamil. I must continue to pay for my lovesick foolishness until I die. But you, Jamil, you have your own destiny to decide. Since you have shown me the kindness of companionship, I will use what little magic I have left to aid you." The elephant's eyes twinkle and glow, then for an instant you feel a breeze blow around the animal. When the glow fades and the breeze quiets, he speaks again. "Your destiny lies beneath these sands. You have but to look a little harder. Go back the way you came, and make certain that your path follows the way of the eagle. Follow the eagle and victory shall be yours."

With that, the elephant raises its trunk, as if sensing the direction. "My home lies that way, Jamil," he says, pointing his trunk to what you believe is the southwest. "May Haku of the Desert Winds keep guard over you."

You watch the elephant trudge across the sand until its form grows smaller and smaller, then you begin to retrace your steps. "Follow the eagle," you mutter. "Eagles don't frequent deserts, and they certainly don't walk across them."

Besides, is it wise to trust a talking elephant?

Turn to 30.

11

You decide to meet the man in the turban. Perhaps he is a wise man who will help you find the third part of the carpet.

As he nears you, he raises a large hand, then motions you to come closer. Cautious, you climb higher until you can make out the features of his face. He is not human!

His face resembles a bull's. Your mouth falls open, and you stare at him, uncertain of what to say or do.

His large brown eyes regard you, and his shaggy brown ears twitch slightly beneath his yellowed turban. A beard, if you could call it that, hangs tangled beneath his bovine lips. Amid the brown and black hair of his beard, you see golden beads braided. They are similar to the beads that ring the top of his staff. The man-bull's wet nostrils flare and wriggle as he sniffs you; the golden ring in his nose shines in the sun.

"Welcome," he says in a deep, rumbling voice. "May peace be upon you, O visitor to my mountain."

"May peace be upon you, also," you reply, remembering the formal Zakharan greeting.

Lifting a long-nailed, humanlike hand, he tugs free the turban to reveal a pair of elongated, curved horns, three silver bells attached to the tip of each. They tinkle softly in the slight breeze. Stuffing the turban in a deep pocket of his dun-colored robe, he continues.

"Sit with Mamoon on his mountainside, share his water, and tell him what brings you here. Your sunbaked skin tells old Mamoon you are far from home." The man-bull tugs on a cord about his waist to pull a flask from the folds of his robe. Uncorking it, he extends it to you. "Water, friend. Please accept my simple gift."

"Yes, thank you!" you say, as you sit on a smooth stone. You drink long and deep. The water is surprisingly cool. You chance to glance down the mountainside to see how far away the man in black is. But he is gone. Puzzling.

You return the man-bull's flask and look into his pool-like eyes.

"Mamoon enjoys having company," the creature says. "A hermit always enjoys having someone to chat with. Tell me, what brings you to my mountain?"

You cannot tear your gaze away from his eyes and find yourself telling the tale of the sea djinni from the beginning. You leave out no details.

"And now I have only two more pieces of the carpet to retrieve," you conclude. "Once I have them, I can

free the king of the Citadel of Ten Thousand Pearls."

"An amazing story, my young friend," the man-bull says. "Djinn are not to be denied. Nor are the Yikaria."

"Yikaria?"

"Yak-men," he replies simply, stretching out his right hand and placing it on your knee. At first the gesture seems friendly, almost comforting, then you realize there is more to his touch. You feel faint, dizzy, your strength ebbing from your body!

You struggle to break free of his grip, but his nails dig into your skin and hold you still. Then his form grows still like a statue, and you feel tingly all over. Tingly and strange.

"Foolish one," you hear the creature speak. In horror, you realize your lips are moving and his words are coming from your mouth. The creature is talking with your voice! "Your young body will serve me nicely," the man-bull's voice continues. "I shall gather the carpet and find the king of the Citadel of Ten Thousand Pearls. I will be wealthy and free of this mountain."

No! you shout, though you find your own voice has no sound to it. You struggle to rise from the mountainside, to get away from the creature and his magic.

"My mind is inside yours," the man-bull speaks again with your voice. "I control your form. It is mine now."

He has control of my body! You suspect he used foul and powerful magic to transfer his essence into your form. You concentrate on making your body stand, but it remains sitting on the side of the mountain. His mind is stronger.

"Do not fight this, Jamil," the man-bull speaks with your voice again. "We share the same body—for now. But soon your spirit will fade to nothingness. And this body will be mine—only mine."

Why? you scream silently.

"I wish to be away from this mountain, Jamil. An outcast, cursed even by my own, evil race—the Yikaria —my bull-like body cannot leave the mountainside. But my new body—your body—*can!*"

Your stolen body rises to its feet, leaving the still form of the man-bull behind. Your hands, under the command of the yak-man, gather up the two sections of the carpet and the magical sword.

"I have a piece of the carpet in my cave," you hear the Yikarian mumble with your voice. "Funny. I never knew it was worth anything. I simply found it one day and have been using it to wipe my feet upon. Ah, soon I shall be rich and free, Jamil."

Yikaria. Yak-men, you think to yourself, trying to remember something from your childhood. As your body climbs toward the top of the mountain, a vague tale from your youth surfaces. You struggle to remember the tale-spinners in the marketplace talking about the creatures, part man, part yak, who are natives of mountains, far away. The creatures cling to the foreboding heights, where they have established an empire built on greed and ruthlessness and power. All those who live nearby fall under the yak-men's dominance. Mothers threaten their misbehaving children that these bogeymen of the mountains will get them if they do not obey. When you were younger, you thought the creatures were make-believe.

"You think too much, Jamil," the Yikarian scolds with your lips. "Yak-men are powerful, but not cursed ones like me. I tried to rule my people, my curious friend. But the others of my kind banded together against me. Fools. Fearful that I would try again, they banished me here."

Where are we?

The Yikarian uses your lips and voice again. "We are far south of the Sheltered River. We are far from the eyes of men. Do not scheme of getting free, Jamil. You are undone."

Glancing up through eyes shared with the evil yak-man, you see the peak of the mountain coming into view. There is a narrow cleft in the rocks, and the yak-man, in control of your body, heads for it.

Beyond the cleft is a cave, and inside it is a crude home furnished with a simple bed and a collection of wooden bowls. The carpet is on the floor. It is dirty and frayed, but it matches the two pieces tucked under your arm.

"For five years I have lived on this mountainside and not realized the carpet was valuable. My means of escape has been in front of my eyes for years. A fool I have been, Jamil."

The yak-man makes your body sit upon the carpet, and holds tight to the other two sections and your weapon.

"How do we make the carpet rise, Jamil?"

I'll not tell the likes of you, you think to yourself. You concentrate on Essaf the Hungry, the Jumlat marketplace—anything to keep your mind away from the carpet.

Carpet. No! His mind is too strong.

"Ah! That is simple!" he cries. "I had but to think of leaving!"

You curse yourself for letting your mind wander to the magic carpet, and you feel your body rise slowly from the rocky floor.

"Stop!" a familiar voice shouts.

Standing in the entrance to the yak-man's cave is the man in black who was following you on the mountainside—the Sha'ir Rashad al-Azzazi!

The only way he could have traced you to this mountainside was through his magic or by coercing the tan djinni in his tower. Your thoughts whirl and intermingle with the puzzled thoughts of the yak-man.

"Out of my way!" the yak-man yells with your voice. "Be gone from my cave!"

The sha'ir strides forward, waggling his fingers and mumbling. You realize he is casting a spell, and the result of his magic is made quickly clear. The carpet settles on the rock floor, and you feel the yak-man's anger grow.

Your body leaps to its feet and draws the magic sword you acquired in the lair of the one-eyed giant. Its blade flashes as your arm waves it back and forth menacingly. It seems the yak-man knows how to fight, you decide as your body crouches into a defensive stance.

The sha'ir comes closer.

"Don't be a fool," Rashad says slowly. "Give me the pieces of the carpet you have collected, and I will spare your pitiful life."

"No!" the yak-man bellows with your voice. He swings the magical sword at the sha'ir. But the sha'ir is nimble, and he dodges the slice. He steps to the side of your body and wiggles his fingers again. A streak of green light shoots from his fingertips and strikes your body squarely in the chest. You hear the yak-man scream in pain with your voice.

Again your arm slashes with the sword, and again you miss, though this time the sword cuts through the sha'ir's fine black clothes.

"You are dead, young pearl diver!" the sha'ir cries. He holds his hands in front of his face, palm outward. A blue glow forms around his fingers. "You are dead!"

Your body falls to the floor, narrowly avoiding a thick blue bolt that sizzles in the air just above you. With a gesture of his hand, the sha'ir casts a spell that wrenches the sword from your hand and flings it far beyond the mouth of the cave.

"You are powerful, stranger!" the yak-man speaks with your voice. "I think your body will serve me better than Jamil's." The yak-man reaches out with your fingers and grabs the sha'ir's ankle. You feel yourself grow faint as the yak-man's mind leaves your body and enters the sha'ir's.

You are free!

A scream fills the small cave.

You are unsure whether the sha'ir or the yak-man is bellowing so, but you don't intend to stay around and find out. You crawl to the carpet and cast a glance back over your shoulder. The sha'ir is wiggling his fingers again and pointing them toward you. Your heart pounds wildly in your chest.

Is it the sha'ir? Or is it the yak-man?

No matter.

Either could kill you. You leap upon the carpet, grab the other two sections lying nearby, and concentrate on freedom. In an instant you are borne aloft, heading down the mountainside.

Faster, faster, you urge, and the carpet responds.

"I'll get you, Jamil! The djinn will be mine!" you hear behind you. The curses continue, but the voice fades as you speed away from the mountain.

Many minutes pass before your heart slows to normal, and, trying to relax, you take a deep breath. Fate was kind, you realize. You could have died on that mountainside—either at the claws of the yak-man or at the hands of the evil sha'ir. Are they still fighting on the mountain? you wonder. If the sha'ir wins, will he find me again?

The questions dance in your head as you speed toward your next destination. You need only one more piece, and the complete map will be yours!

Turn to 20.

12

The giant two-headed roc chatters to you as it flies you down the side of the mountain.

"Left or right of the giant you should stay," the female warns. "To his sides he has much difficulty seeing."

Listen to her. If you stand right in front of him you will be dead.

You shiver, and not just from the chill evening air.

The roc's flight takes you nearly to the bottom of the mountainside. The bird hovers outside a cleft in the cliff face. You now understand why the two-headed bird has not fought the giant in its home. The cave is little more than five feet wide, but it is easily fifteen feet tall—too narrow for the roc.

The two-headed bird deposits you outside the cave, and the female beak nudges you forward. You see only blackness beyond, and you hesitate.

"Man, you must move. Inside you must go," the female urges. "Kill the giant."

"How can I hope to see in there? It's black as midnight. And how do I know the giant is inside?"

"Listen closely," the male head instructs.

You comply, and over the rustling of palm leaves you hear snoring.

The female head whispers. "Sleeps, he does. Inside you must sneak. While he snores, slay him."

You edge toward the mouth of the cave and grasp the spear with both hands. The soft twinkling from the spearhead grows brighter in the darkness, providing nearly as much light as a lantern. Truly this weapon would fetch a fine price in the Jumlat marketplace.

The cave floor is littered with debris. Bits of bone from who-knows-what-animals, chunks of shells from the roc's stolen eggs, rotten fruit, and feathers encrusted with dried blood are strewn about everywhere. Carefully picking your way between the bits of refuse, you edge deeper inside—toward the sleeping giant. The snores become louder the farther you travel, and the

sound bounces off the cave walls, making it difficult to
tell where the noise is coming from.

Ahead, the tunnel widens into a crude room filled
with makeshift furniture. The stench of spoiled meat
and fruit hangs heavy in the air, making the chamber
seem close and decidedly uncomfortable.

A giant-sized chair has been fashioned from pieces of
a ship's mast, and a sail covers the seat like a cushion.
Four kegs with planks laid across them serve as a table.
From the marks on the kegs you can tell that this wreckage came from more than one ship. The weathered paint
on one barrel reads, "*Al-Nisr*," meaning "*The Eagle*." You
pause. *The Eagle* was a ship lost in the Crowded Sea more
than a year ago, returning from one of its runs to cities
dotting the coast along the Foreigners' Sea.

Glancing up, you see that bones and a scattering of
golden-brown feathers cover the top of the table, which is
eye level to you. In the center of the table is a ship's
lantern—the large kind that hang from the prow. The rest
of the room is a collection of hunks of wood, bands of

metal from barrels, and swatches of material from previous visitors. Cloaked by the shadows of the cave is a large cage, also fashioned from ship parts. Stepping closer, you shudder and see an ape slumping lifelessly inside.

Beyond, the cave tunnel continues, as does the snoring. Taking a deep breath, you slightly stoop, amble under the table, and stalk forward. You then notice that the eyes of the caged ape follow your every movement, and the animal tries to pull itself to a sitting position. A sad cry from the ape roots you to the stone floor.

The snoring stops.

Sniff. Sniff. You hear from the darkened chamber ahead. "I smell an intruder. Heh, heh, heh. A bedtime snack."

For an instant you consider running back the way you came. But you are certain the two-headed roc is waiting, and you know it can surely best you.

Gripping the spear more tightly, you step backward until you are under the makeshift table again, then squint as bright light suddenly fills the stony chamber.

The giant strides into the room, carrying a ship's lantern in one hand, and a large club in the other. The giant is at least three times your height. His dun-colored, muscular frame glistens in the lantern light. His only clothing is a loincloth made from a ship's sail. A mane of unkempt reddish hair sticks out from his head at all angles, and his large, single eye, red with sleep, glares malevolently. He sets down the lantern, gazes about the room, and his eye fixes on the moaning ape.

The giant grunts and shrugs, apparently oblivious to your presence. He takes a step toward the caged animal, and it howls pitifully, scrambling to reach the back of its crude cell.

"Quiet, breakfast!" the giant barks in a gravelly voice. "I was trying to sleep." He bangs his club against the cage for emphasis and turns to go back into his chamber.

One step.

Two.

He stops and sniffs the air.

"I *did* smell an intruder!" he bellows, whirls, and

stoops to look under the table. With a speed you are
surprised he can muster, he tips over the table, sending
the lantern, bones, and feathers everywhere and leaving you out in the open.

The ape howls mournfully as you stare wide-eyed,
and the giant closes in for the kill. He raises the club
and aims at you, pulling back for a mighty swing. Just
in time, you roll to the side and hear the sound of
wood splintering. The giant just demolished his chair.

"Flea!" he bellows, the word echoing about the
chamber. "You'll be a dead flea!" He pulls free his club
and shoulders it for another swing. "You'll be my bedtime snack!"

You jump to your feet and dodge another swing.
The force behind his blow is incredible and ruffles
your hair as if you were caught in a strong breeze.

He strides forward, and you lunge between his legs,
coming up behind him and thrusting at his back with
your spear.

"No!" you cry as your weapon breaks against his
tough hide and does nothing more than scratch him.

"Heh, heh, heh. My evening snack wants to play. I
like to play with my food before I eat it."

The giant turns to face you. He moves slowly, knowing that you are weaponless. He flicks a dirty hand
forward and bats you as if swatting a bug. You fly backward across the chamber and land soundly on your
rump. The wind is knocked from your lungs and you
sit momentarily stunned as the giant closes.

"Little snack. Don't put up a fight. I'll swallow you
quick. It won't hurt much."

You swiftly gaze about the chamber, looking for a
place to hide or something to use as a weapon. You realize it would be hopeless to bolt out the way you came in.
The giant could reach you in one step, and there would
also be the two-headed roc to contend with.

The giant shoulders his club and takes another step
forward. He grins broadly, revealing a row of filthy
yellow teeth. Hefting the club in his right hand, he
raises it above you and brings it down.

Summoning all your strength, you push yourself to the side and feel a tremor as the club crashes against the cave floor where you were. The club's end splinters from the force of the blow, and the giant howls in rage.

"Little snack, stay put!"

Remembering the roc's advice, you dance to the giant's right side, nimbly moving about to keep him from looking directly at you. The roc's words seem true, as the giant turns his head about until you are in front of his eye.

"Flea!" he blusters again, and swings so vigorously that you feel the air move out of the club's way.

Jumping behind him, you spy something that might suffice as a weapon. It is a rusty gaff hook, likely taken by the giant with the rest of his ships' souvenirs. You sprint toward the hook, close both hands about it, and then dance to the side. Again the giant's club lands where you stood but a second ago.

"Stop playing, flea!"

You leap to his left and swing the hook, just as the club hits soundly on the stone floor again. This time the whole club shatters, and slivers of wood fly at your feet. In the same instant the hook finds its mark, its point lodging in the fleshy part of the giant's left thigh.

The giant howls in pain and flails his arms around, attempting to dislodge the weapon.

Undaunted and spurred on by success, you pull the hook free and swing it again, this time striking him in the back of his leg. The giant's howls reverberate through the chamber, and you cringe from the excruciating noise. However, this time his flailing hands find the source of his pain. His thick, dirty fingers close about the hook.

"No!" you shout, knowing that if the giant gains your weapon, you are done for. With your fists beating furiously at his hand, you force him to release the hook, and you quickly pull it free. Blood spills from the giant's wound, and he growls in anger and pain.

"This flea can sting!" you brag, pivoting to the giant's right side, narrowly missing his hammerlike fist. Trying a new tactic, you swing the hook at his foot, easily finding your mark.

"Aarrgh!" the giant screams and doubles over to grab the hook.

In one motion you pull the hook free again and swing it upward, lodging the rusty point squarely in the giant's chest, where your own heart would be.

"This flea bites hard!" you exclaim, proud of yourself.

His single eye fixes on you with a stare of disbelief. His hands grab at the hook, but his fingers wiggle uncontrollably. You jump back just as he falls to his knees, then pitches forward.

His great body takes in a few last gulps of air, then he shudders once and lies still.

Falling backward on your rump, you wipe the sweat from your brow and take several deep breaths. You have never killed anything before, and although you are smug at your victory over the giant, you feel oddly sad. He may have been evil—or he might have been only following his instincts to survive.

Rising from the floor, you turn toward the whimpering ape and pad to its cage. You'll free the ape, but if he challenges you, he should not be difficult to beat, not after you bested a giant. You tug the bar free and open the door. The ape slowly clambers out, cries once, and lumbers sluggishly out of the room toward the cave mouth.

"My good deed for the day," you whisper. "Now to get out of here."

You could follow the ape, tell the giant two-headed roc its enemy is dead, and order it to fly you home. Or you could explore the cave, the chamber the giant came from. Perhaps there are bits of this and that the giant kept from the ships he looted. As you ponder the possibilities, you hear a muffled cry from the cave entrance. The ape!

"Food!" you hear one of the roc's heads call.

"A tasty ape!" the other announces.

You sigh. At least the ape's end would come quickly. Deciding to explore the other chamber before facing the roc, you angle the giant's lantern so you can see into the room beyond. His bed was little more than a

crude collection of sails and blankets, stitched together
with rope and stuffed with baby roc feathers. The bedding is dirty, likely never seeing a washing, and dotted
with the husks of insects the size of your palm.

Convincing yourself there must be something of
value here, you poke around under the cloth and feathers until you meet resistance. Carefully reaching under
the bedding, your fingers find a wooden box. It is as
long as an oar, yet no more than six inches deep or
wide. You gingerly pull it free of the bed.

Tugging the box into the other chamber where the
light is better, you see faint words, "Fayiz." So, this box
and what is inside belonged to someone named Fayiz.

"Fayiz probably is dead. And even if he isn't he
won't be needing what is inside," you whisper. Throwing open the box, you frown. Inside is a rusty cutlass
lying atop a rolled-up rug that is likely in worse shape
than the giant's bed. You set aside the cutlass and reach
for the rug. Perhaps something valuable is tucked
away inside it.

You unroll the rug, and dust balls dance in front of
you. You sneeze several times and rub your eyes. The
rug is old, though not so worn as you first suspected. It
is made of woven reds and purples, muted through
age or by design—it is hard to tell. Intermingled with
the red threads are bits of gold. Pure gold. They catch
the light from the lantern. Studying the golden threads,
you can tell they make up an intricate design, being
solid lines in some places, doted lines in others. They
crisscross over the red and purple threads.

The threads are frayed on one end of the carpet, as if
the carpet had been cut in two. Examining it closely,
you are certain that the carpet had been larger at one
time. You dig about under the bed, hoping to find the
other half. But your efforts are futile.

Stepping back from the rug, you see the designs a
little differently. The red patterns appear to be islands,
and the purple, the sea. The Crowded Sea? There are
certainly islands you recognize from your travels pearl
diving. The rest of the picture is unknown, cut off with

the rest of the carpet. You search the giant's cave for several long minutes, hoping to find the other section of the rug, but again you come up empty-handed.

You stare at the gold threads. Perhaps they mark a course, a path some great adventurer took ages ago. Perhaps you could follow the threads and discover some great treasure at their end.

No, you remind yourself. Adventures are for heroes. You refused to help the marid because you are not the heroic type. Better to live a safe life that is not filled with surprises and fights with giant creatures.

Suddenly the rug rises a few inches from the floor and hovers. Your mouth gapes open in surprise.

"It is a flying carpet!" you exclaim. "My chance to get home!"

You move to sit on the carpet, but stop yourself and grab the cutlass. The rust falls off the blade like dust. The weapon is beautiful, a blade crafted of the finest silver and edged with pure gold. Reverently, your hands close about the hilt. It fits your fingers perfectly, as if it were made just for you.

I am the Cutlass of the Golden Gulf, you hear the blade sing. *I am yours. Wield me well.*

Surprised and frightened, you drop the blade, and it clatters on the stone floor.

Ouch! it cries. *Pick me up at once!*

A magical carpet and a magical sword!

You bend and pick up the weapon, flashing the blade about in the chamber, feeling its balance and watching the weapon reflect the light. The more you handle it, the more accustomed you get to it. Along its pommel are runes, expert etchings of fish, shells, and starfish. Still grasping the hilt, you run the fingers of your other hand over the engraved images, and the blade speaks to you again.

My powers are great, and are yours to command. With me in hand, you can dive into the greatest depths of the seas and breathe water as if it were air. With me in your hand, you can swim as well as any fish.

Your mind races. As a pearl diver, you would be able

to stay underwater as long as you wanted, never needing a boat or a rope boy to pull you up. In fact, you could start your own pearling operation. No longer will you have to scrape out a meager living.

You hold the cutlass and sit squarely on the hovering carpet.

"I am yours to command, master," the rug speaks.

Talking weapons. Talking birds. Talking giants. Talking rugs. Indeed the Land of Fate is a wondrous place.

"Shall I fly you away from here?" the carpet asks. "I am old and have only enough magic left in me for one trip."

Rubbing your chin, you agree. After all, you have to get off the island somehow. And leaving by walking out the way you came in—where a two-headed roc might be waiting to either honor its word or eat you in spite of the bargain—probably isn't the best idea in Zakhara.

"Master, shall I take you home?" the carpet queries.

"Home sounds awfully good about now," you decide.

The edges of the rug flutter, sending more dust everywhere. Slowly, slowly, you magically rise from the cave floor. The carpet rotates once, circles the chamber, and exits the cave, flying past an astonished two-headed roc.

Soaring over the night-drenched island, you climb higher and higher, where the air is chill. The stars are out—myriad and twinkling and shining, showing you the way home.

The air washes over your face, and you grin. Today has been a challenge, one you don't want to repeat. After all, you are a pearl diver, a man who makes his living from the Golden Gulf.

By dawn you see the towers and flags of Jumlat, City of Multitudes. The pearl boats are just readying their crews for a long day's work. Beyond them you see the marketplace, and your magic carpet flies you over the brightly colored stalls. Soon there will be throngs of people about, buying and selling wares and telling each other tales and humorous stories.

Farther, farther you fly—into your bedroom window.

Tired, you roll up the carpet, place it under your bed, and drift off to sleep to dream of the adventure you might have had if you had aided the green djinni.

THE END

13

Your arms ache, yet you move them as rapidly as possible, propelling your scrap of wood toward the ship. It is your salvation! You kick your legs with all of the energy you can summon, and you pray to Haku that you can reach the ship before it moves away.

After what seems like an eternity, you are closer to the vessel. Fate has smiled upon you, for it appears the ship is headed toward you. Still, you are too small for those on board to notice you. Gathering what is left of your strength, you resume your swim toward the ship.

You are close enough now that you can make out some of the vessel's details. She is a fine ship, with crisp sails and newly painted trim. You can see a bevy of sailors scrubbing the rails and working on the rigging.

You wave your arms to gain their attention, but a call for help dies on your lips when you see what is painted on the side of the ship.

You can just barely make out the ship's name, artistically rendered in light blue paint—*Rahat's Dagger*. No! The *Dagger* is a pirate ship. Her captain and crew are the scourge of the Golden Gulf! They are known for looting pearling ships and merchant vessels. Fortunately, you know they are not murderers. The captain has a reputation for leaving those who surrender unharmed.

Your mind reels. What to do. What to do.

You glance to the north and spy the outline of the shore. Perhaps you have enough strength to swim to land after all. Maybe no one on board the pirate ship has spotted you, and you can swim away undetected. But perhaps you will drown trying.

Or, perhaps catching the pirates' attention would

not be a bad thing. It is said the captain does not hurt those who yield to him. And you are exhausted.

If Fate guides you toward the island, turn to 23.
If you trust yourself to the pirates and signal the ship, flip to 17.

14

Surely agreeing to fight the giant would be jumping from the frying pan into the fire. You can't win by strength, but perhaps by wits. The two-headed roc is intelligent enough to speak, and therefore perhaps you can trick it into arguing with itself, letting you escape.

"No," you state, your mind made up. "I will not fight the giant. That struggle is yours. It is your family that is being menaced."

The female head screeches in anger. "Too little to be our champion, I told you he was. Have a brave heart he does not!"

The male head nods solemnly, and before you can set your plan in action, its beak grasps you about the waist. The great creature pivots in its nest and holds you out to the trio of two-headed baby birds. You realize the giant bird has won: you are to be dinner for its young.

You pray to Haku your end will be swift. The sharp beaks strike out at your body and you mercifully lose consciousness.

THE END

15

You will not be so foolish as to chase after a giant bird carrying an elephant!

There's no use looking for trouble. Hah! Why look for trouble when it seems trouble easily finds you?

Happy that you made the right decision, you whirl and retrace your steps. It is easy to see where you came from. The hot breeze is so slight it does not disturb the sand, and you can clearly see your footprints.

You pause. If you can see your tracks, the roc could, too. When it finishes eating the elephant it might come looking for you as a snack.

Tearing off a piece of your linen robe, you swish it over the sand behind you, erasing your trail.

You are a smart one, Jamil! Now all you have to do is find the final section of this carpet. It is tiring carrying the three pieces you already have with you. The rug is thick and heavy. Why some old sha'ir would make a treasure map out of a flying carpet—and then tear that carpet into four pieces—is beyond you. It would have been easier to make a small map, one that is not heavy and one that you would not have to race across the Land of Fate trying to assemble.

You pick up your pace, wanting to put as much distance as possible between you and the huge roc. As you go, your eyes dart back and forth across the horizon, looking for some clue—something you overlooked earlier.

If nothing else, perhaps you will come across the riders and they will offer you some water for your parched throat. Indeed, you are very thirsty.

Turn to 30.

16

The large yellow warehouse is freshly painted. You can smell it, and you note drops of paint on the ground outside of the door. You have friends in Jumlat whose homes look worse than this storage building. The warehouse looks clean and prim, and there is not a bit of debris around it.

You reach forward and open the warehouse door, confident that your goal is close at hand. Instantly, a hundred smells assault your nostrils. You identify cinnamon, jasmine, orange, coffee, and vanilla. Your eyes water from the intense scents that fill a small, cluttered office.

"May I help you?"

The speaker is beautiful, with a voice as soft as a spring day and hair the color of polished copper. She sits behind a desk littered with scrolls and sheets of parchment. Her bright-blue eyes peer curiously over a transparent pink veil. The rest of her outfit, a common robe that looks anything but common on her, is a darker shade of pink. You find yourself staring at her.

"I said, may I help you?"

"Y-Yes," you stutter. You blush and finger the sleeve of your djinni-designed caftan. "I'm looking for a bottle. A blue one."

"Try the market. We only store goods for merchants. We don't sell anything."

"Oh, it's a very specific bottle. If I wanted a bottle—any bottle—I would not be troubling such a busy person as yourself. And I'm not looking to *buy* this bottle," you explain, standing tall and looking her straight in the eye. You smooth the wrinkles from your garment and run a hand through your hair. "It's a very long story. But to make it short, I don't even really want the

bottle, just what's inside it."

The girl glances at you curiously, then tugs free an almost barren sheet of vellum and reaches for a quill.

"This bottle is stored with us?"

"Yes," you state authoritatively.

"Can you describe it and name the merchant who owns it. We will have to contact him about your interest."

You give her a puzzled look. When you came in this building, you didn't think getting the bottle would be so complicated. Of course, you have never been in a warehouse before. You scratch your chin and notice that she is smiling at you—likely amused. She looks even more beautiful when she smiles.

You could tell her the entire story, hoping she believes you and is sympathetic enough to help. Or, you could come back after dark and find the bottle yourself. That might be easier.

"Listen," she states, interrupting your musings. "We store spices mostly, for the merchants coming into the city. We hold them here for up to a few weeks until they are shipped inland. We have a small number of other items stored here, including, perhaps, the bottle you are so interested in. But my aunt, Kila Odani, manages this warehouse. And I don't think she'd like it much if I let strangers wander around inside looking for someone else's property."

You pace in front of her desk, then whirl and place your hands on the only empty spot. Now is the time to make a decision.

Do you tell her why you are so interested in the bottle? One so attractive as she must be honest and caring. If this is your course, turn to 42.

Do you fabricate a story, one that will gain you the bottle without revealing the truth about the sea djinn and the evil sha'ir? If so, flip to 32.

Or do you decide to return at night, sneak inside when the workers are gone, and attempt to find the bottle that way? If so, turn to 39.

17

The pirates are not murderers, you remind yourself. You're better off trying to catch their attention than risking a long paddle to land. You'll simply convince them to drop you off at the closest port.

Your decision is made. You will trust your luck to the pirates. You struggle to kneel on the piece of wood and nearly plunge into the water. Still, you manage to balance yourself, and you begin waving your arms about frantically and, in a scratchy voice, calling out for help.

Haku be praised! One of the sailors spots you. He points in your direction, and other sailors move toward the ship's rail. After what seems like hours, the great ship eases near. You are helped on board by several pairs of strong, callused hands.

"Look what we caught, Cap'n!"

"Jamil," you whisper. "My name is Jamil. From Jumlat."

"Well, you're a long way from the City of Multitudes, boy!" The chuckling captain measures well over six feet tall. He is barrel chested and bronzed from the sun, and he is attired in jade-green pants, expensive from the look of the material, and an embroidered white linen vest that is stained with blood. Three thick gold chains hang about his neck and hold your attention for a moment. Then he moves. His considerable muscles ripple beneath the fine fabric, and you feel the deck creak as his bare feet move across it.

Strapped to his side is a polished and oiled scimitar that gleams in the afternoon sun. Its hilt is as black as the curly hair that frames his scarred face.

"Well, well, mates," the captain continues. "What should we do with him? He's small. Maybe we should throw him back and let him grow bigger."

The crew laughs heartily.

"No, I think we'll keep him a while," the captain says, "if he can earn his keep. Sintar! See if he can fight!"

A man not much bigger than you bounds in front of
the captain. He draws a thick-bladed sword and with a
flourish waves it at the air before you. For a moment
you're not sure what to do, then you find a similar
sword thrust into your hand by one of the seamen.

"Defend yourself, Jamil!" the captain bellows.

The man in front of you waves his sword again and
nimbly jumps forward. You duck just in time as his
blade thrusts where your face was but a second ago.
The crew cheers, and your attacker darts toward you
again, this time slashing with his weapon. The blade
makes a swishing sound as it cuts through the air. You
jump aside and hear a "thunk," as the sword tip strikes
the deck. The man is trying his best to kill you!

"Dance, Jamil!" the captain cries. "Dance for your life!"

The stories say these pirates are not killers, your
mind declares. But yet again your assailant swings his
blade, and again you dodge it.

This time you bring your borrowed weapon into
play, extending it away from your body to keep the
swordsman from getting too near. The weight of the

weapon is good. It is well balanced. You try a few slashes with it while your opponent darts in behind you. If you had not spent days adrift at sea, no doubt you could wield it better.

You whirl to face him and instinctively bring your weapon up to parry his. His blow is strong and nearly knocks your blade away, but you persevere and grasp the hilt more forcefully. You know that if you were not so tired you would have the energy to handle this duel. It is taking all of your fading strength just to keep him from slicing you into pieces.

"Get him, Sintar!" one of the seamen shouts to your opponent. "Draw blood!"

Sintar responds by raising his sword high above his head, meaning to bring it down upon you. In response you jump to the side and swing your own weapon at him, slicing it in a sideways arc that cuts through his flesh just above his waist.

The pirate howls and drops his weapon, lifting both hands to his wound, as if trying to keep the blood inside. Pleased with yourself, you close in for the kill. But you are roughly stopped by several pairs of hands that hold you in place and take the sword from your fingers.

"Enough, Jamil!" the captain barks. "Sintar was only playing with you. If he'd truly been fighting, you would be dead." He strides through the crowd of sailors and inspects Sintar's wound. "It's not deep. He'll live. Get him below and treat the cut."

The captain pivots toward you. The expression on his face is difficult to read. Is he angry at you? He grabs the black hilt of his scimitar, and you tremble. Then he throws back his head and chuckles.

"Well, Jamil. You've passed our test. You're certainly fit to join the crew of *Rahat's Dagger*. But you'll need some sword practice." He nods over his shoulder and barks an order to one of his men. "Get him some water, clean him up, then bring him to my cabin. I want to learn about Jamil from Jumlat."

Your bath is quick, but refreshing. Though you are still exhausted from your days adrift, you are not given any time to rest or eat. A pair of pirates escorts you to the captain's quarters.

"Mind your tongue and manners around Captain Ahmad, lad—or you won't have a tongue for long." Laughing, the larger of the two brusquely shoves you inside. You had hoped for better treatment from your rescuers. Well, at least you are alive. The door slams shut behind you.

The captain's cabin is filled with odds and ends, sea chests, sextants, and all manner of objects from other ships. A small strongbox near a table sits open—filled with strings of pearls, large sapphires, and shining pieces of gold that hold your gaze.

"Like my prizes, lad?" the captain asks, drawing your attention to the other end of the room. His large frame seems too big for the carved ebony chair he sits in. Perhaps he ordered his furniture so he could appear imposing. "Someday a share of all this could be yours. Of course, you'll have to work hard for it."

He rises and pads toward you. "First, Jamil, I want to know what brings you to my sea. If your ship's nearby perhaps I'll attack it and find something on it to add to my trophies."

You explain about the marid, and how you freed her. You spare no details. As you finish your tale, the captain pitches back his head and laughs loud and long, a deep belly-laugh that reveals yellowed teeth and a scar that runs nearly all the way across his neck.

"Never anger a djinni, lad, especially a powerful one. Not unless you have the magic or the sword arm to back up your words—and I can tell you certainly haven't the former." Pausing, he paces about the treasure-cramped room and laughs again. "You will stay on my ship, Jamil. I've need of a young man to clean the decks, repair the rigging, and tidy up after the cook. As you grow older and more accustomed to the sea, I'll teach you to fight like a real pirate."

A life at sea? Living as a pirate?

"No!" you shout. "Let me off at the next port! You can't kidnap me!"

The captain laughs again. "Kidnap you? Why, Jamil, you asked to come aboard my ship, remember? We saved your life, and you are indebted to us. Think of working for me as paying off that debt. It will take a long, long time to pay it off."

Your hopes of returning to Jumlat are dashed.

Resigned to your fate, you nod to the captain. He turns you over to his first mate, who gives you the tools of your new trade—a mop and a pail.

THE END

18

I'd rather take my chances with the giant than become bird food, you think to yourself. Besides, once I leave the bird's nest, I could escape. The sun is setting. I can slip away into the trees below, and it won't see me. I'll slip away in the darkness.

Despite your thoughts and your plan for escape, you announce aloud to the two-headed roc, "I will be happy to serve as your champion and kill the giant!"

Satisfied, the female head squawks at the baby birds, and they waddle back against the far side of the nest. Their hungry beaks snap at the air.

"Apes for dinner we will feed them," she informs you. "Too valuable you are to serve as food."

The male head's beady eyes glare at you. "But you must be careful, man," he warns. "Will you be careful? The giant is tricky. He has only one eye but is strong, sneaky, and much, much larger than you. We've seen him use a club that can smash stones into pebbles."

The female head strains forward and pokes through the thatching of the nest. A moment later, her beak retrieves a spear. From where the bird was poking, something sparkling catches your eye, jewelry, no doubt—souvenirs from the bird's two-legged meals.

"This fine sticker you can use," she instructs. "Against us a man once tried to use it."

"He was delicious," the male head recalls.

Taking the spear, you notice it is light and well balanced. An exquisitely fashioned weapon, its point twinkles blue. Magic, perhaps? You hope so. If so it will fetch a fine price in the Jumlat marketplace, where you hope to be as soon as possible.

"Well, I must be going down the mountain, then," you state, starting to climb out of the nest.

The female head lunges forward, and her beak grabs you gently about the waist.

The male speaks. "We will take you to the mouth of the cave, then wait outside."

"That's not necessary," you argue. "Don't you think you should stay here and protect your babies? I'm certain I can find the giant's cave on my own."

The male head shakes back and forth. "We want to make sure you fight the giant and don't fool us and run away."

Your plans for escape are squashed, and you resign yourself to a fight with a one-eyed giant. You feel yourself being lifted as the wings of the two-headed bird flap strongly to take the creature into the air.

The sun has set, taking with it the last semblance of warmth from the sky. You shiver and your teeth chatter. Hopefully the cave will be warmer.

Turn to 12.

19

You stare at the giant, magically suspended in time. If the spell that holds him ends, his club could come down upon your head.

You glance at the green djinni.

"All right, Tala. I'll help you. I'll try to find your husband. After all, I don't have much choice in the matter," you say.

"You are wise, Jamil the pearl diver, Jamil my champion."

The marid winks and grabs you by the hand. You feel yourself being lifted from the forest floor.

You rise among the trunks of the massive palms and glance below. The giant shakes the effects of the magic from his befuddled brain and slams his club to the ground where you stood only moments before. He would have killed you. You took the only correct course of action.

Still, working for this marid might bring about your death as well. She flies you from the island, like a bird without wings. At first you are afraid as her course takes the pair of you higher and higher. However, when you are certain she will not drop you, you begin to enjoy the sensation of the air rushing over your skin. The sea looks like a painting from your bird's-eye view. It is still and beautiful, and the waves are tiny white flecks. Ahead and below you see the shores of Zakhara, the Land of Fate. The buildings of Jumlat, your home city, look like a toy village, small and fragile and unreal. As you glide closer, you squint to make out the antlike forms of people. The great marketplace—there it is. Colorful tents and awnings dot the ground, and antlike people scurry about.

You fly north of your city, tracing the coastline. The Bountiful Shoals, a fisherman's delight, lies ahead, its coral reefs making the water appear orange and yellow in places. You wonder if the oysters there are filled with pearls.

Your musings are interrupted as the green djinni angles her course to the northwest. "There, Jamil!" the marid cries. "Ahead is Sikak, called City of Coins. In the heart of the city is the evil sha'ir's tower. And inside the tower you will find the bottle that traps my husband."

Through a break in the buildings you spy the Al-Nuhas River, the River of Copper. Indeed, from this high up its waters glitter like coins. Perhaps this is how proud Sikak got its name. The marid takes your path lower, and the ground rushes up to meet you. She steers the two of you toward a small grove of trees just south of the city, and there she sets you down. The earth feels good beneath your feet, and you almost lose your balance on it as she lets go of your hand.

"Look, my champion!" the marid states, pointing through the trees. "See the rose-colored tower? The one apart from all the other tall buildings?"

You nod, still entranced by the sights of the City of Coins.

"That is the sha'ir's tower. Sha'ir Rashad al-Azzazi. The human who dared to rob sixty years from my husband and me, the human who dared to confine our power." Her voice is sharp and bitter, and as she continues, you note that her skin becomes a darker green.

The marid turns her gaze to you, and her emerald eyes flash indignantly. "Well, what are you waiting for, Jamil? There is his tower. Now, go rescue my husband, the king of the Citadel of Ten Thousand Pearls. Hurry. I will wait for you here. If you are not back by nightfall, I will come search for you. But be warned, Jamil the pearl diver, I will not confront the sha'ir to save you. Even I fear his power, and I do not wish to be confined in a bottle for another six decades."

With that, you strike off toward the tower, pondering how you will find the bottle and rescue the marid's husband from a sha'ir who is probably long dead.

Turn to 24.

20

The carpet whisks you away from the mountain, the sha'ir, and the yak-man.

You travel for hours high above the Land of Fate, watching the mountains and trees rush by.

The carpet slows as you approach a desert. The sand below is dotted with small oases, but the carpet's course takes you beyond the hospitable havens. The carpet skims on, angling lower still until you are barely three feet above the sand. The desert is vast and beautiful, but its heat can be deadly.

Lower still the carpet flies until you feel the heat of the sand beneath the fabric. Suddenly the carpet stops, dropping you a few inches to the desert floor.

All you can see is sand and bright blue sky. The sun overhead indicates late afternoon. You are tired and hot, but you are determined to find the final piece of carpet. But where to look?

All you see is sand, sand, and more sand . . . and a shimmering patch of something in the distance.

It is unfortunate the carpet did not deposit you closer to another of its sections. You are thirsty, tired, and the heat of the desert will make you want water and rest very soon. You opt to walk toward the shimmering ground, lugging your carpet sections with you. Unfortunately you are weaponless, your wondrous magical sword left on a rocky mountainside many, many miles away. Better the sword was left behind than your life.

Perhaps there is water where the air shimmers, you think as you walk. Or perhaps the glimmer is an illusion created by the heat. You must find out.

Half an hour later you seem only a little closer to the shimmering spot. It could be a pool of water. It looks faintly blue.

While you continue to ponder what it is, something new catches your eye. You spy a cloud of sand. Horsemen, you suspect, and they are not far away. There are not many, judging by the size of the sand cloud that rises to cloak their forms, but they seem to be moving quickly in the midday heat. That is odd, as most people travel in the desert in the early morning and early evening hours.

It seems you are faced with more choices, Jamil.

Do you walk toward the shimmering spot? It might be a mirage, or water. If this is your path, turn to 26.

Or do you wait for the riders? Nomads are said to be hospitable, and perhaps they have water and tales to share. If this is your decision, turn to 36.

21

Fighting a monstrous, two-headed bird would be foolish, you decide.

You flee from the creature, darting into the safety of the grove beyond the clearing. Behind you, the bird squawks furiously, apparently angry that a meal has eluded it. You breathe easy and stare at the bird, confident that you are safe.

Although the trees are huge and their canopy high overhead, they are close enough together to keep the giant bird from pursuing you. The creature would only tangle its wings, and you would escape.

You watch as it circles in the clearing, its beaks snapping irately. Suddenly, the thing flies toward the trees, and for an instant you fear it will try to catch you despite the protection of the jungle. But it arcs skyward at the last moment, and you relax when you no longer see it.

The light is diminished in the woods, and the longer you travel, the darker it becomes. You know it will not be long before nightfall. Deciding to put some distance between yourself and the clearing, you strike off again, the soft melodies of the parrots and the chirping of insects keeping you company. You angle your course toward the mountain. Surely you will come across some sign of civilization there.

You travel for an hour before stopping to look about. The hairs on the back of your neck stand up, and you feel oddly nervous. Something is wrong, but you can't seem to identify the problem. You get the sense someone—or something—is watching you. But you don't even hear a snapping twig to indicate a watcher.

That's it! You don't hear anything. The forest here is unnaturally quiet. You don't see any of the colorful parrots you noted earlier, and you don't hear any insects. They were scared off by something. But what?

Well, I'm not going to stand here to find out, you decide. Lengthening your stride, you move toward the mountain and run into a hairy tree trunk.

Hairy tree trunk?

The giant's legs are as thick as trees, though not as tall. They block your path as surely as any wall would. You are knee-level to the giant, staring straight into his ugly, hairy, muscular, and massive knees. Your gaze travels upward, and you gasp in surprise when you take in all of the creature. The giant is nearly three times your height, and he is wider around at the waist than any of these trees. Dirty and brawny, he grins down at you with a single dull-gray eye that sits in the middle of his low forehead.

His teeth are uneven and broken, as is the club in his right hand. Still, the piece of wood looks like a formidable weapon. And he looks like a more-than-formidable foe.

"Heh, heh, heh. A little man," the giant chuckles in a booming, gravelly voice.

He can talk!

Maybe I can reason with him! Maybe he's not dangerous, you think, as you fall soundly on your behind at the stamp of his foot.

"Heh, heh, heh. A little snack!"

All right, no chance to reason with him, you conclude, wondering if everything on this island is out to eat you.

He reaches a grime-smeared hand toward you. Frightened and flustered, you grope about for your dagger. Just as your trembling hand closes about the hilt, his fingers circle your waist and lift you.

"Yum," the giant gushes, the reverberating sounds filling the air. "Don't fight, little snack. I'll swallow you quick. You not feel anything."

Swinging wildly with your dagger, you stab into the back of his hand. Roaring with more surprise than pain, he drops you and cradles his wound.

"Little snack bites back! Bad little snack."

The fall momentarily stuns you, and before you can scramble away, he is towering over you again, his broken club aimed at your prone body. "I'll kill the little snack!"

"Stop!" cries a familiar voice.

The giant hovers above you, motionless, as if magically suspended in time.

Scrabbling out from under his shadow, you pull yourself to your feet and look about for this new menace. There she is, sitting coyly on the branch of a young palm. Tala, the marid, the one who is responsible for getting you into this predicament. This time she is only five feet tall.

"Jamil," the djinni coos. "Aren't you even going to thank me?"

You notice that above water her skin is also green, nearly the color of the palm leaves. Her seafoam-colored hair hangs about her shoulders, waving like the leaves in the slight breeze.

"Thank you?" you sputter. "It's because of you that I'm here!"

"And it's because of me that you are not squashed flat amid the ferns. I doubt our giant friend would have missed you. On the other hand, I *have* missed you, Jamil, my champion. And I've decided to give you another chance to help me." She floats like a feather to the ground and steals quietly toward you, her emerald eyes flashing with anger or amusement. You can't decide which.

"My husband is still trapped in a bottle, as I was before you freed me. You must help me find him and free him, too, Jamil." She smiles. "Of course, if you're still not interested in helping me, I can find another champion. You'll still have the giant to contend with. It is your choice, Jamil. What will you do?"

Do you agree to rescue the green djinni's husband despite the terrible danger entailed? If this is your destiny, turn to 19.

Or, would you rather try to best the giant than battle a sorcerer? If so, Fate takes you to 4.

22

"My master does not like trespassers," the djinni scolds as she unfolds her legs and stands before you. She closes her eyes and the world spins around you. When the dizziness stops, you notice your surroundings have changed—drastically.

You are in an opulent room with carved furniture draped in silks and piled with satin and velvet pillows. The air smells faintly of frankincense, and you hear birds tweeting sweetly. Dozens of bright yellow and orange birds flit about in white wooden cages that hang from the ceiling. In the center of the room, a fountain bubbles in front of a rich-looking divan.

Seated on it is an imposing man with a braided black beard. The man is dressed in a robe dotted with jewels; the garment must be worth the price of a large pearling ship! On his head he wears a turban with an emerald clasp as big as your fist. His fingers are adorned up to the knuckles with gold and silver rings. His eyes are neither blue nor black, but some whirling, hypnotizing combination of the two colors. They are active, lively eyes that take in everything. Using the arm of the divan for support, he rises and faces the tan djinni.

"Master," she gushes, as she falls to her knees. "O most powerful Sha'ir Rashad al-Azzazi, greatest wizard in all of Sikak, I bring a trespasser. Jamil is his name. I caught him sneaking up the back stairway."

The sha'ir stares at the djinni for several long moments, then turns his attention to you. "So, Jamil, you have come here to steal from me, that is certain. But what you want to steal, I can't fathom. My wealth is guarded far too well for the likes of you."

The sha'ir begins to pace, indicating with a flick of his wrist that the tan djinni should rise.

"What to do with you, Jamil? What to do?" He fingers his beard, then turns on his heels. "Where are you from, Jamil?"

"Jumlat," you state cautiously, figuring that bit of knowledge should evoke no punishment.

"Jumlat on the Golden Gulf," the sha'ir sneers. "Well, Jamil. I think I shall send you far from home—and far from the sea. I'll not worry that you'll try to steal from me again. My dear djinni, if you will . . . ?"

"Of course, Master," the tan djinni replies.

And once again the world spins around you, the colors of the room swirling before your eyes, melting together like the fabric-painters' dye in the Jumlat marketplace. The air grows warmer as the colors blend together and fade, and the scent of frankincense vanishes.

When the motion stops, you find yourself sprawled in the sand, the hot grains grinding into your hands and face. You spit out a mouthful of sand, squint your eyes into the merciless sun and scan the horizon.

Sand.

Nothing but sand all around you.

Struggling to stand, you feel the heat flow over your body. From the sun's position it is noon. But noon where? Zakhara has so much desert you could be anywhere. Perhaps if you had told the tan djinni the truth, you wouldn't be in this predicament. Perhaps you should never have opened the marid's bottle in the wreck in the Golden Gulf.

Self-pity and hindsight will do you no good now, you chide yourself. You pick a direction, what you believe to be south, and start walking.

You will make it home, you realize, for you are too stubborn to give in. But it will be a long while before you see the gleaming spires of the City of Multitudes. You will not be wealthy. You will not have rescued the king of the Citadel of Ten Thousand Pearls. But you will have your freedom, and you will be safe. And those are priceless gifts.

THE END

23

I will paddle toward the land instead of the ship, you decide. I just hope I have enough strength to make it.

You settle astride the piece of wood, letting it keep your body afloat, and you paddle with your arms, propelling yourself toward the tree line. From time to time, you stop to rest and close your eyes, forcing out the glare of the sun on the water.

You must have fallen asleep during one of your rests, for when you open your eyes it is late afternoon. The sun has started its journey toward the horizon. Fortunately, the breeze and current have carried you closer to the land. Now that you are nearer, you can tell the land is an island.

Paddling again, you reach the shore just before sunset. The island is lush and beautiful. A virtual paradise in a vast sea, its enchanting blossoms, colorful parrots, and cool breezes tug your mind away from your problems. But nothing calms your stomach. It rumbles annoyingly and sends you in search of food and water. You pass by a bush laden with fat red berries. You scoop handfuls of them into your mouth and continue onward.

You travel nearly half a mile inland when you find a clear stream shaded by giant palms. You bathe in the cool, sweet water, drink your fill, wash your loincloth, and sleep until dawn. Your rumbling stomach wakens you, and you sate your appetite with nearby dates the size of your fist and more of the large, succulent berries.

Now that you are full and rested you can pay more attention to your surroundings. Aside from being on an island somewhere, you have no idea where you are. Perhaps this is an isle in the Crowded Sea, the great body of water that feeds into the Golden Gulf.

The trees are huge, and the colorful parrots are as large as eagles. You wonder if the island is inhabited by men—or monsters. Some islands in the Crowded Sea are said to be the home of djinn. You hope this one isn't. You've had your fill of magic and djinn.

Well, you will find out soon enough if this island is home to something other than parrots. You put on your clean, dry loincloth, then fashion slippers from plant leaves and tie them about your ankles with supple vine. You keep three dates for later and make sure you still have your curved dagger. Satisfied you are ready for anything, you set off deeper into the foliage.

You hike for most of the day, noticing that the trees get even larger the farther inland you travel. Some of the palms are so great that you could not wrap your arms about their trunks. The bushes are unusually large, too. Perhaps frequent rains and warm breezes nurture the island.

A break in the trees lets you peer between the palms to a low mountain in the distance. The sun hovers above the peak, signaling evening is only a few hours away. Perhaps on the other side of the mountain there is a port where you can find a ship that will take you back to Jumlat.

Hoping to find just that, you continue on. Shortly before sunset you pass beyond the thickest of the bushes and enter a clearing filled with waist-high dark green grass. There are more trees, perhaps even larger ones, on the other side.

You pull a date from your pocket, take a bite, and stop in midchew as if you were a statue. A shadow has just passed over the clearing, sending shivers racing down your spine. It is the shadow of a giant two-headed bird. The bird is as large as a pearling ship, and you quiver in amazement and fear.

Gasping in surprise and regaining your senses, you blink skyward and stare in disbelief at the thing. How could something so large fly? One of its heads looks down to return your stare, and you drop the other piece of date from your trembling fingers. With a horrifying cry, the creature banks and plummets toward the clearing, its beaks open wide.

It is at once terrifying and beautiful, the brown and gold feathers on its wings ruffling as it plunges. Its massive heads are covered with dense orange and crimson feathers, and its dark yellow beaks turn to black toward the curved tips. The twin beaks clack together menacingly as the bird swoops closer.

You still have your curved dagger. You could fight the creature with it, you think, though you worry if the huge beast would even feel the sting from the small blade. Or, you could run toward the trees and hope to outrace the thing.

You must make a decision quickly.

Do you stay in the clearing to fight the giant bird? Worse menaces might lie in the trees beyond. If you fight, turn to 25.
Or do you run toward the trees, hoping the beast cannot follow? If so, turn to 21.

24

It takes you nearly an hour to traverse the crowded streets of Sikak leading to the rose-colored tower. Along the way you "borrow" a linen robe that someone had hung out to dry. No use traveling through the city in a loincloth—it might draw unwanted attention.

The robe is a little big, but it will have to do. The hem of your garment drags on the cobblestones as you reach the rose-colored tower.

The tower is an old building; the rosy-hued stones stretch a dozen levels above the ground. You imagine that at one time the stones were resplendent, for when you look close you can see flecks of metallic black and silver in them. Now, however, the stones are faded with the decades.

You edge closer to one of the tower's doors.

Of course, Sha'ir Rashad al-Azzazi, who snared the two djinn sixty years ago, is probably dead, and his relatives likely live here now. The more you think about it, the more confident you become that he is long gone and buried. After all, if he was old that long ago, he must be dust and bones by now.

But the big question is whether the tower's current owners will let you glide right in and search for a special bottle.

What will you say to them? "Hello, my name is Jamil. I'm a pearl diver, but I've been asked by this beautiful green djinni to rescue her husband. He might be inside in an old bottle. Do you mind if I look around?"

They'll believe you.

When elephants fly.

"Mother, I will be back in a few hours. There's some fabric I want to buy in the marketplace."

The words snap you to attention. They come from a lovely young woman who is leaving by the tower's side door. The woman's clothes and bearing mark her as a servant. The door, then, must lead to the tower's work areas and servants' quarters.

This is your way in! Sneaking inside seems more reasonable than explaining about Tala and her trapped husband and a sha'ir who thrust them in bottles six decades ago.

Clinging to the morning's shadows that fall gently about the tower, you reach the door. You listen carefully to make sure no one is just beyond, and you tug at the handle and pull the door open.

The kitchen lies before you. It is filled with fresh fruits and vegetables, and a trio of cooks are hard at work preparing the midday meal. They labor over lamb meat, chopping and seasoning it. A servant woman stokes a fire. Watching them makes you hungry. But you have things more important than food on your mind.

Beyond the cooks is an open door that leads deeper inside the tower. And nearby is a wooden stairway ascending into darkness. As you ponder which route to take, one of the cooks turns to you, knife in hand.

"Ah, the delivery boy. Put the dates in this corner," he says, gesturing near the cook fire with his knife. "Don't leave them to sit outside. They will draw flies." Without another word, he returns to chopping the lamb meat.

Taking advantage of the situation, you withdraw through the door you just came in to make the cooks think you went outside to get the dates. After a sufficient pause, you enter again and scramble up the wooden stairway. Who knows where this will take you? At the very least, it will take you away from the servant woman and the cooks with the big knives.

Up, up you climb, passing two landings without doors. Why did I get involved in this? you berate yourself. If someone catches me in here trespassing I could be thrown in prison—or worse. Maybe I should leave and tell Tala I can't find the bottle. That wouldn't be a lie. I certainly haven't found it so far.

Your mind continues to dance with questions as you climb higher still.

"Stop!" a female voice commands.

You do just that, but you see no one in front of you. Turning your head, you glance down the stairway. It, too, is empty. Perhaps the voice came from the other side of this wall and you are simply overhearing a conversation.

You cautiously take another step.

"I said stop."

The voice comes from above you! You throw back your head and see a comely young woman sitting cross-legged in the air above you. Judging by the sandy color of her skin and her purple, piercing eyes, she is a djinni of some sort. She wears a silky garment that barely covers her torso, and leggings that are sheer and billowy.

"Who are you, little trespasser?"

You stare at her.

"Do you have a tongue, man?" the djinni persists, resting her elbows on her knees and staring at you curiously.

"Jamil," you state, swallowing hard. "I'm not a trespasser."

"Well, Jamil, my master has no servants by that name. So I suspect you are here unbidden. And that makes you a trespasser. Perhaps you are trying to steal into his harem. Or perhaps you are a thief trying to steal some of his jewels. Tell me, Jamil, what brings you to Sha'ir Rashad al-Azzazi's tower? What brings you to the home of the most powerful sha'ir in the City of Coins?"

The sha'ir *is* alive! your mind screams. What to do? What to say? You could run—back down the stairs and out through the kitchen, losing yourself in the Sikak marketplace. You could tell her the truth and pray she does not kill you or call the sha'ir. Or you could create a clever lie, an excuse for climbing the back stairway of Rashad al-Azzazi's tower. Thinking quickly, which do you do?

Tell the djinni you are here to rescue your sister from the sha'ir's harem? If so, turn to 2.

Tell the djinni the truth about Tala and her captured husband? If this is your action, turn to 9.

Flee back down the stairs? If your feet carry you in this direction, turn to 27.

25

I will not run, you declare. I will face the giant two-headed bird. Summoning your wits and bravery, you step into the center of the clearing and draw your curved dagger.

The bird's cries pierce the sky like a crack of thunder. The noise seems to make the very ground shake. Resolute, you brandish your dagger and swing it in a broad arc as the great two-headed bird closes.

Squawk! shriek the heads in unison as the thing dives toward you. The right beak clacks loudly, mere inches from your head, and you fall prone into the tall grass to avoid a lunge from the left beak. So much for fighting this bird, you think. *I can't get past the heads to even hurt the beast.*

The heads scream, angry that their meal eluded them. You feel the ground quake, and you realize the bird has landed. The grass all about you rustles as the heads poke here and there looking for you.

You pick yourself off the ground and crouch amid the grass. The curved dagger is in your hand, ready. You could run toward the other side of the clearing and the safety of the trees, but the bird is probably faster. You could slink along on your belly like a snake, hoping the bird won't find you. But the moving grass would mark your passage. *I could stand and fight like a man,* you remind yourself.

The bird moves closer. You can feel the tremors in the ground with each step it takes. It is closing in on your hiding place. You hold your breath, hoping it won't hear you, while you try to decide what to do.

Squawk! Squawk! the thing cries. The noise is so loud you drop your dagger and cup your sweating palms over your ears.

Squawk!

A persistent head pokes through the tall grass, and its moon-shaped eyes stare at you. The giant-sized bird has found you! It cries again, and your hands do nothing to drown out the deafening sound.

Reacting quickly, you fall flat to the ground, grab your dagger, and roll to the side. A beak furiously closes upon air behind you. Jumping to your feet, you rush toward the bird, past its necks and right up to its underbelly.

You crouch beneath its body, between its legs. You move with the bird as its heads continue to hunt for you amid the grass. You have outwitted the thing by hiding under its very body!

The great creature continues to squawk and search. If you survive this, will you become deaf? Certainly it has to give up sometime and fly home. But the bird is stubborn. It cries and squawks and stamps the grass flat in its pursuit of dinner.

I have to do something. Anything, you think. I can't hide under this bird forever. Maybe I can kill the thing. Grasping the hilt of your dagger in both hands, you thrust upward. The blade slides through feathers and sinks into the flesh of the bird's belly.

The heads scream, sounding almost human. The giant-sized bird flaps its wings and rises a dozen feet above the clearing, with your dagger imbedded in its belly.

The grass all around you has been stomped flat by the bird's massive claws. You are weaponless and in the open. Taking a deep breath, you sprint toward the trees. Your feet pound over the earth.

Then suddenly your feet have nothing to stand on. The wind is knocked from you by a scaly claw that closes about your body and carries you aloft. The bird has caught you and lifted you from the ground! Your legs dangle uselessly, as if you were a doll being carried by a rough child.

The bird's wings beat strongly, and the breeze they create chills you and causes your eyes to water as if you were crying. Clenching your teeth, you pray that death will come swiftly and without pain.

Higher and higher the great bird carries you, clearing all of the massive palms and letting you catch a glimpse of the shoreline in the distance. As it continues to rise, its wings take it toward the mountain. Why the bird did not eat you in the clearing is a puzzlement, a question you fear to ponder as you look at the tops of the trees far below. From your vantage point, you can see a good portion of the island. It is large, and the sole mountain in the middle of it is covered with dense

vegetation. You see no villages or ports.

The bird angles its feathery body toward the mountain peak, crying with both of its heads as it nears its destination. You twist your body so you can see better, and your heart skips several beats. The bird is gliding toward an immense nest—filled with a trio of two-headed baby birds. Though they appear newly hatched, the baby birds are much larger than you! And they look hungry!

Gathering its wings close to its body, the mother bird plummets, then unfolds her wings above the nest to hover and gently coast to the babies. The great bird lands silently, her claw releases you, and you fall into the twigs and leaves that make up the nest. The giant bird moves closer to the young birds, then turns one head backward to watch you.

"Little person," you are startled to hear the head speak. "A fine dinner you will make for my babies." The voice is feminine, though not at all pleasant.

"Hmm. *Your* babies?" the other head squawks in a male voice several octaves lower. This head also turns to look at you. "*Our* babies! You think everything belongs to you." Satisfied it has corrected its other half, the male head tucks in close to its body, and the beak feels about the stomach until it finds the hilt of your dagger. With one tug the dagger comes free and drops into the nest. There is little blood on the blade, evidence you barely hurt the creature.

"*Our* babies. Yes," the female head says icily. "A filling meal the little person will make for our babies."

"No!" you screech. Being torn apart by a half-dozen hungry bird heads is not how you want to die.

"Dinner the little man does not want to be," the female head says.

"Hmmm. Then perhaps we could offer the meal an alternative," the male replies.

You stand, stunned that two heads belonging to the same bird could carry on a conversation. Perhaps while they squabble you could dive over the side of the gigantic nest and escape. You take one step. Two.

Three. . . .

"Ouch!" you squeal as one of the young birds nips at your bottom. You were so engrossed in the talking giant bird you did not notice its young moving in.

"Wait for dinner you must, my baby," the mother head scolds. "Talk with your dinner, we wish to do first."

"Yes, t-t-t-talk," you stutter, attempting to discourage the two-headed creature from feeding its babies. Diving out of the nest apparently isn't an option. And being digested by two-headed young does not pose a bright future. "Wh-Wh-What kind of creature are you?"

The great bird interposes itself between you and the young, and the male head moves closer until its beak is only inches from your chest. "We are a roc, of course."

"A two-headed roc we are," the female interjects.

"And we have a proposition for you," the male continues. "Are you listening? Hmmm?"

You nod fervently.

The female head takes a turn. "Bothers us does a giant."

"Bothers us?! Vexes us! Tasks us! Is our bane! Ruins our family! Destroys our home!" the male corrects.

"Quiet! Speaking I am," the left head snaps. "Our eggs he steals and our young he kills when we are away hunting. Our nest he tears apart. Too big we are to hide ourself from his sight. Comes to our nest he does when we fly away for food. Comes to our nest he does and takes our babies."

"We nearly caught him once," the right head interrupts. "But he ran down the mountainside and darted inside his cave. We cannot fit inside the cave. We are too big."

"But fit *you* could," the female says evenly, squinting her beady black eyes.

"You could go inside and kill him," the right agrees. "But if you are not up to the task, you certainly will be up to dinner."

"Well, little person," the female begins. "Our champion will you be? Or dinner will you be for our babies?"

Do you refuse to fight the giant, thinking it would be easier to escape the roc than slay a giant? If so, turn to 14.

Or do you agree to fight the giant, hoping the giant is less formidable than the roc? If this is your destiny, turn to 18.

26

You arrive where you had seen the shimmering water, but find only hot sand. Squatting and digging your fingers into the grains and sifting through them, you find no trace of moisture. A cursed mirage! In your heart you knew there would be no water; such are the tricks of the Zakharan desert.

Standing, you wipe the sweat from your brow with the back of your hand and notice your skin is hot to the touch, burned by the merciless sun. You would welcome Essaf the Hungry's salves and ointments now, and your dry lips would welcome even a few drops of water. Why is Fate against you?

Staring ahead, you again see something shimmering against the ground in the distance, near a bowl-shaped depression. The shimmering is blue and inviting, like water pushed by a desert breeze. Perhaps this is real water—water that will slake your thirst. Or perhaps it is another mirage.

You could press on, or you could turn around and hope to find the riders whose sand cloud you noticed half an hour ago. Another piece of the carpet has to be around here somewhere. It must! There simply has to be something here other than hot, white sand.

Cursing and grinding your heels into the coarse grains, you notice a huge shadow fall across your path, cooling you for the briefest of moments.

Throwing your head back, you see what caused it. A great roc, with a wingspan wider than Essaf's pearling boat, glides on the hot breeze. In one of its claws it carries an elephant that trumpets shrilly in pain and fear.

You are outside the giant bird's notice—at least for the moment. Perhaps you are too small for it to even see you. Still, it would do you no good to stay out in the open, risking that the bird will think you a dessert to sweeten its belly after finishing the elephant. Your eyes follow its course, and you notice it is heading to where the desert slopes downward, near the bowl-shaped depression next to the water you spotted earlier.

What to do, what to do?

Do you press on to the shimmering sand where the roc came to rest? Perhaps the piece of the carpet you seek is there. If you think so, turn to 10.

Or, do you retrace your steps, searching the sands to see if you missed a clue to the fourth piece of carpet. If this is your action, turn to 15.

27

The djinni hovers above you. You doubt you could lie convincingly to her. And you suspect she wouldn't believe the truth.

Besides, there's no use taking chances with the whims of a djinni. You nimbly whirl on your heels, hike your linen robe up so you won't trip, and you sprint down the wooden stairs.

Two steps at a time. Your feet fly forward to hit the last step when you find yourself nose to nose with the tan djinni.

"Time to visit my master, I think," she scolds. "The sha'ir likes to chat with trespassers—before he kills them."

Turn to 22.

28

You quickly decide to take the djinni's advice. You shudder to think what the sha'ir could do to you. You flop cross-legged on the carpet and it rises of its own volition.

"Stop!" the sha'ir fumes. His fingers begin to glow as he mumbles something you cannot understand, perhaps a spell.

You don't stop. You probably couldn't if you wanted to. The carpet flutters forward, and the sha'ir is forced to duck or be knocked over by it.

"Ryea, my favored djinni, get him!" you hear the sha'ir bellow behind you.

Your breathing quickens, and you begin to panic. "Hurry, hurry," you whisper to yourself. The next moment, the carpet picks up speed to follow your directions. "Great Haku!" you shriek, grabbing the sides of the rug and holding on tight. Once secured, you order, "Faster!"

The carpet zips through the rooms beyond, sending servants falling to the floor and harem girls fleeing.

"There, a window!" you direct, and the carpet flies outside and over the buildings of Sikak. Glancing back at the tower, you see the angry sha'ir leaning out the window and shaking his fist at you.

"South," you state, intending to travel to the marid and tell her about the sections of the map and the dead sha'ir's treasure trove.

But this time the carpet does not respond. Instead, it flies to the west, leaving Sikak, City of Coins, behind.

"No. Stop, carpet! Stop," you bark. But your orders continue to go unheeded. "Where is this thing taking me?!" Your knuckles turn white from gripping the sides of the rug so tightly.

"Please stop. Please!"

You feel like you are a child's toy, being pulled by an invisible string to some unknown destination. For hours the carpet flies, passing over cities, desert, and trees. You grow tired and eventually nod off to sleep, curling on the carpet and praying to Haku that you won't fall off.

You awake in the morning over water, probably the Crowded Sea, you think. There are several islands ahead, and the carpet seems headed toward the smallest of them.

"Of course!" you exclaim. "I forgot that this carpet would take me to the other pieces." You finally relax and take in your surroundings.

The carpet angles downward now, pointing itself toward a mountainside crowded with riotous, junglelike growth. Down it flutters, depositing you on the ground amidst gigantic palms about a third of the way up the side of the mountain. The vegetation is huge. The trees seem impossibly tall, and their trunks are thicker than an elephant's stomach. Perhaps magic is at work here. Plants can't normally grow so massive, can they? Still, the plants are not your concern right now.

Glancing upward, you see an opening in the side of the mountain—a cave mouth that is nearly twenty feet tall. Yet, it is narrow, and it looks like a black slit between trees and vines. Something about the cave calls you. Another piece of the carpet must be inside.

You roll up your rug and tuck it under your arm. Grabbing for support on to a vine as thick as your forearm, you start your climb toward the cave mouth. As you go, you think about the frightened tan djinni and the evil sha'ir. You didn't set out this morning to be a hero and save the marid king, but now that you're headed along that path, you have no regrets. Men as evil as the sha'ir have no right to imprison anyone.

The blackness within the cave opening is darker than the sha'ir's beady eyes. After stepping inside, you close your eyes for a moment to let them gradually adjust to the darkness, a trick you learned from diving on cloudy days. In time, you open your eyes and pad forward for a moment, then stop. Did you hear something? The trickle of water? Rocks falling? You listen more closely and let your eyes adjust more.

No. Snoring. You hear snoring. Someone—or some-*thing*—is sleeping inside this cave.

You inch deeper into the darkness and stumble over a piece of wood. You freeze like a statue, pausing to see if anyone heard you. No. The snoring continues.

Feeling along the floor, your fingers grasp a wooden shaft. You follow the smooth shaft until you feel a point. It is a spear. Groping along the floor of the cave, you notice other spears, though these are broken. The cave floor is littered with debris. Bits of bone from who-knows-what-animals, chunks of thick shells from giant-sized eggs, feathers stained with dried blood, and rotten fruit lie everywhere. Carefully picking yourself up off the floor, you grab the unbroken spear and step carefully between the bits of refuse as you edge deeper inside.

You carefully stash your carpet near the cave mouth and move in deeper, your spear at the ready. Who knows what could be snoring so loudly? The snores become louder still the farther you travel, and the sound reverberates off the cave walls.

Ahead, the tunnel widens into a crude room filled with makeshift furniture. It is dimly lit by a massive lantern hanging from the ceiling. The stench of rotten meat and fruit hangs heavy in the air, making the chamber seem close and uncomfortable.

A giant-sized chair has been fashioned from pieces of a ship's mast, and a sail covers the seat like a cushion. Nearby, four kegs with planks laid across them serve as a table. From the marks on the kegs, you discern that this wreckage came from more than one ship. The weathered paint on one barrel reads, *The Eagle*. You pause. You know that *The Eagle*, a Jumlat vessel, was lost in the Crowded Sea more than a year ago, returning from one of its runs to the coast of Bahr Al-Ajami, the Foreigners' Sea.

Glancing up, you see that bones and a scattering of golden-brown feathers cover the top of the table, which is eye level to you. The rest of the room is filled with hunks of wood, bands of metal from barrels, and swatches of material. Cloaked by the shadows of the cave is a large cage, also fashioned from pirated ship parts. Stepping closer, you shudder and see a listless ape inside. Quietly searching the room, you discover no sign of the other piece of the carpet. Still, you know it must be here.

Beyond, the cave tunnel continues, as does the snoring. Taking a deep breath, you stoop slightly, amble under the table, and stalk forward.

Whatever lives here is big. Very big.

The eyes of the caged ape follow your every movement. A sad cry from the ape roots you to the stone floor.

The snoring stops.

Sniff. Sniff. You hear from the darkened chamber ahead. "I smell an intruder. Heh, heh, heh. A bedtime snack."

For an instant you consider running back the way you came. But you are certain another section of the carpet is in this cave, and you must have it. Gripping the spear more tightly, you step backward until you are under the makeshift table again, then squint as bright light suddenly fills the stony chamber.

A giant strides into the room, one hand carrying a ship's lantern nearly as big as you, and the other bearing a large club. The giant is at least three times your height. His dun-colored, muscular frame glistens in the lantern light. His only clothing is a loincloth made from a ship's sail. A mane of unkempt reddish hair sticks out from his head at all angles, and his large, single eye, red with sleep, glares malevolently. A cyclops! He sets down the lantern, gazes about the room, and his eye fixes on the moaning ape.

The giant grunts and shrugs, apparently oblivious to your presence. He takes a step toward the caged animal, and it howls pitifully, scrambling to reach the back of its crude cell.

"Quiet, breakfast!" the giant barks in a gravelly voice. "I was trying to sleep." He bangs his club against the cage for emphasis and turns to go back into his chamber.

One step.

Two.

He stops and sniffs the air.

"I *did* smell an intruder!" he bellows, whirls, and stoops to look under the table. With a speed you are surprised he can muster, he tips over the table, sending the lantern, bones, and feathers flying and leaving you out in the open.

The ape howls mournfully as you stare wide-eyed, and the giant closes in for the kill. He raises the club and aims at you, pulling back for a mighty swing. Just in time, you roll to the side, and you hear the sound of wood splintering. The giant just demolished his chair.

"Flea!" he bellows, the word echoing about the chamber. "You'll be dead, flea!" He shoulders his club for another swing. "You'll be my bedtime snack!"

You jump to your feet, nearly tripping, and dodge another swing. The force behind his blow is incredible, and it ruffles your hair as if you were caught in a strong breeze.

He strides forward, and you lunge between his legs, coming up behind him and thrusting at his back with your spear.

"No!" you cry, as your weapon breaks against his tough hide and does nothing more than scratch him.

"Heh, heh, heh. My evening snack wants to play. I like to play with my food before I eat it."

The giant turns to face you. He moves slowly, knowing you are now weaponless. He flicks a dirty hand forward and strikes you as if swatting a bug, and you fly backward across the chamber and land soundly on your rump. The wind is knocked from your lungs, and you sit stunned as the giant closes.

"Little snack. Don't put up a fight. I'll swallow you quick. It won't hurt much."

You swiftly gaze about the chamber, looking for a hiding place or a weapon. You realize it would be hopeless to bolt out the way you came in. The giant could reach you in one step.

The giant shoulders his club and takes another step forward. He grins broadly, revealing a row of filthy yellow teeth. Hefting the club in his right hand, he raises it above you and brings it down.

Summoning all your strength, you push yourself to the side and feel a tremor as the club crashes against the cave floor where you were. The club's end cracks from the force of the blow, and the giant howls in rage.

"Little snack, stay put!"

You dance to the giant's right side, nimbly moving about to keep him from looking directly at you. The giant turns his head about until you are in front of his eye. So! He cannot see well to his sides. This could work to your advantage!

"Flea!" he blusters again, and swings so vigorously that you feel the air move out of the club's way.

Jumping behind him, you spy something that might suffice as a weapon. It is a rusty gaff hook, likely taken with the rest of his ships' souvenirs. You sprint toward the hook, close both hands about it, and then dance to the side. Again the giant's club lands where you stood but a second ago.

"Stop playing, flea!"

You leap to his left and swing the hook, just as the club hits soundly on the stone floor. This time, the club splits in two and slivers of wood fly at your feet. In the same instant the hook finds its mark, its point lodging in the fleshy part of the giant's thigh. He howls in pain and flails his arms around, attempting to dislodge the weapon.

Undaunted, and spurred on by your success, you pull the hook free and swing it again, this time striking the giant in the back of his leg. The giant's howls reverberate throughout the chamber, and you cringe from the excruciating noise. However, this time his flailing hands find the source of the pain. His thick, dirty fingers close about the hook.

"No!" you shout, knowing that if the giant gains your weapon, you are done for. Beating furiously at his hand with your fists, you force him to release the hook, and you quickly pull it free. Blood spills from the giant's wound, and he growls in anger and pain.

"This flea can sting!" you brag, pivoting to the giant's right side, narrowly missing his hammerlike fist. Trying a new tactic, you swing the hook at his foot, easily finding your mark.

"Arrgh!" the giant screams and doubles over to grab the hook.

In one motion, you pull it free and swing it upward, lodging it squarely in the giant's chest.

"This flea bites hard!" you exclaim proudly.

His single eye fixes on you with a stare of disbelief. His hands grab at the hook, but he can't seem to dislodge the weapon. You jump back just as he falls to his knees, then pitches forward. His great body takes in a few last gulps of air, then he shudders once and lies still.

Falling backward on your rump, you wipe the sweat from your brow and take several deep breaths. Although you are elated at your victory over the giant, at the same time you feel oddly sad. He may have been evil, or he might have been only following his instincts to survive.

Rising from the floor, you turn toward the whimpering ape and pad to its cage. You'll free the ape, but if he challenges you, he should not be difficult to beat—not after you bested a giant. You tug the bar free and open the door. The ape slowly clambers out, cries once, and lumbers sluggishly out of the room toward the cave mouth.

"My good deed for the day," you whisper.

Deciding to search for the second piece of the carpet, you step into the room beyond to explore. The giant's bed was little more than a crude collection of sails and blankets, stitched together with rope and stuffed with who-knows-what. The bedding is dirty, likely never seeing a washing, and dotted with the husks of insects the size of your hand.

You convince yourself there must be something of value here, and you prod under the cloths until you meet resistance. Carefully reaching under the bedding, your fingers find a wooden box. Long as an oar, yet no more than six inches deep or wide, you gingerly pull it free of the bed.

Tugging the box into the other chamber, where the light is better, you see faint words, "Fayiz—*The Eagle*." So, this box and what is inside belonged to someone named Fayiz, who sailed on *The Eagle*.

"Fayiz probably is dead. And even if he isn't, he won't be needing what is inside," you whisper. Throwing open the box, you grin broadly. Inside is a rolled-up rug—one that matches the carpet that flew you here—and a rusty cutlass. You lay out the magical rug and step back from it. You notice designs, probably similar to the designs on the rug that brought you here.

You stare at this piece, noting red patterns that appear to be islands, and a large swath of purple, which must be the Crowded Sea. You pad to the entrance of the cave, where you left the other piece, bring it back, and try to match up the two sections.

No. They don't connect. Obviously you need another fragment before you can begin to make any sense of the thing. You roll up the first section, move to sit on the one you just acquired, then you stop yourself.

The cutlass! It might come in handy.

You grab the hilt and gasp as the rust falls away like dust. The weapon is beautiful, a blade crafted of the finest silver and edged with pure gold. The hilt fits your fingers perfectly, as if it were made just for you.

I am the Cutlass of the Golden Gulf, you hear the blade sing inside your head. *I am yours. Wield me well*.

Surprised and frightened, you drop the blade, and it clatters on the stone floor.

Ouch! it cries. *Pick me up at once!*

A magical carpet and a magical sword!

You cautiously bend over and pick up the weapon. After a few moments of silence, you are confident it will not harm you. Lifting the weapon, you swing it about in the air, feeling its balance and watching the weapon catch and hold the light. The more you handle it, the more accustomed you get to it. Along its pommel are runes, expert etchings of fish, shells, and starfish. You run the fingers of your other hand over the engraved images, and the blade speaks to you again.

My powers are great and are yours to command. With me in hand, you can dive to the greatest depths of the seas and breathe water as if it were air. With me in hand, you can swim as well as any fish. Powerful am I. Sharp and strong.

And you just might save my life, you say to yourself as you sit upon the carpet. It rises from the floor unbidden and floats out of the cave and down the mountainside. You realize it is taking you to the third piece of carpet.

Hopefully a one-eyed giant won't be guarding it.

Turn to 3.

29

You decide to face the sha'ir. After all, you are certain he could use his magic to catch up with you before you could seek refuge with the turbaned man.

You whirl and draw the magic sword from the folds of the carpet and let the pieces of the carpet fall to the rocky ground. You grasp the hilt of the sword with both hands and point the tip toward him.

"Stay away!" you cry.

He continues to climb the side of the mountain, an evil grin spreading across his face.

"I don't want to fight you. Stay back!"

"I'll have that carpet, thief," the sha'ir growls. He stops several yards away and puts his hands on his hips. "Give me the pieces of my grandfather's carpet, and I'll let you live. Refuse, and I'll kill you."

Would he really kill you over two pieces of a rug? Does he have the power to kill you? After all, you have a magical sword.

He is giving you a choice. Fight him or surrender the carpet. What should you do?

Do you relinquish the two sections of carpet, giving up your quest to save the king of the Citadel of Ten Thousand Pearls? If so, turn to 34.

Or do you stand your ground and fight if necessary? This choice leads you to 31.

30

You pad over the fiery sands. The coarse grains rub against your feet. One step. Two.

You struggle to keep your balance as your feet sink deep into the sand. Past your ankles. Past your calves. You continue to be swallowed by the warm grains. Then your feet strike something hard. But that substance, too, gives way beneath your feet, and suddenly you find yourself plummeting in darkness—blackness.

It is as if you have been swallowed whole! Musty air closes in all about you as grains of sand fall upon your head! You swing your arms and legs about wildly, hoping to find something to grasp on to so you can stop your fall. In the process, you drop your pieces of carpet.

For an instant, the fingers of your right hand strike a rocky ledge. You grasp it and struggle to hold on, but the rock is too smooth, and your fingers slide down its surface. You flail about with your other hand, trying to find the rock again. But your actions are futile, and you continue your plunge into the darkness.

Your fall is long and comes to a painful end on a hard, cool bed of sand. The wind is knocked from you, and your arms and legs ache from the impact. You lie still for a moment to make sure you are all right, then you slowly tilt your head up.

Light spills in from far, far overhead—the hole you stepped through. You let your eyes become accustomed to the dim interior and look around. You are inside a vast chamber with rocky walls that stretch a hundred feet toward the desert floor above.

Carefully picking yourself up off your gritty cushion, you stretch your limbs to reassure yourself that nothing is broken.

"Where am I?" you ask, noting a slight echo in the

chamber. "Where I am supposed to be, I guess," you answer, glancing at the sections of the rug that fell through the hole with you.

I bet the fourth piece of carpet is somewhere down here, you think to yourself. All I have to do is find it, and it will fly me out of here. You study the rocky walls of the cavern. They are too sheer and canted; you could not hope to climb them. Well, if I can't find the carpet, I'm likely to die here, you think glumly. Maybe its buried under my feet.

You kneel and dig like a persistent dog through the sand for more than an hour and, though your fingers bleed from the effort, at last you are rewarded. You have found something—several somethings—beneath the coarse sand. You pull the items free one by one and are abruptly struck with revulsion. Bones! You've found the remains of other desert travelers who were unlucky enough to fall into this cavern.

Bones and cutlasses and nothing else. You grasp the hilt of one of the swords and feel its balanced weight. Nothing special. You drop it.

There has to be more.

Digging further, you unearth a lantern, still nearly full of oil. Working feverishly, you coax a flame from its wick so you can better view your surroundings. It is fortunate you found such a prize, as you can tell from the little light that spills in from overhead that the sun is setting in the desert above. The lantern and swords are old, perhaps resting on the cavern floor for decades. And the bones—picked clean by insects and who-knows-what-else—might as well be ageless.

"By the caliph's jewels!" you howl in frustration. "There is no carpet here. There is nothing but death." Rising and pacing, you scatter the bones with your feet and grasp the lantern angrily. You mutter a curse to all djinn and evil sha'irs and glance upward toward the hole. No way out.

There is barely enough oil in the lantern to last through the night. You take another trip about the chamber and inadvertently spot an opening in the cavern wall, a darkened passage you thought at first glance was only a shadow. Was it there before and you did not notice it? Or did it just appear?

You move closer to the opening, and you peer into the darkness. Well, since you can't climb out, you might as well see what lies this way. You grab up your three sections of carpet, tuck them under your arm, and grip the lantern securely. Swallowing hard, you take a step into the passage. The flame from the lantern reflects from the uneven stone walls, which sparkle in places. Sparkle? Your gaze catches a shiny spot. There is moisture on the cavern walls! Reaching your empty hand to the rock, you feel the coolness of damp rock, and you bring some of the moisture to your lips and sweating forehead. For several long minutes you do this to cool your parched skin. Feeling a little better, you continue down the mysterious passage, hoping it will lead you to the last part of the carpet and a way out of this place.

The air is still, damp, and stale with age. An unpleasant odor assaults your nose, but you ignore it and press onward, the light from the lantern reflecting hauntingly off the walls, chasing away the shadows, and revealing—something. There, in the glint of the lantern light, the wall reflects warmly back.

Gold. The walls contain veins of gold! The precious metal holds the lantern light and beckons you closer.

"I'd surely be a caliph if I could mine these veins," you whisper, entranced by the thoughts of riches. Yet you realize you haven't the tools—or the time. Sighing, you continue your trek through the underground tunnel, vowing that if you succeed in finding the carpet, you will come back here someday—with the proper tools and a few of your pearl-diving friends to provide the needed labor. Of course, you'll first have to find out just where you are.

Ahead the light diverges, split between the entrances of two chambers. The entrance to the chamber on your right is carved and decorated with bits of stone to resemble the open mouth of a serpent; pointed rocks hanging down from the top of the passage look like uneven fangs. Squinting upward, you can tell that the beast's eyes are set with large, smooth pieces of jade that must be worth a small fortune. Beyond the mouth you see only shadows.

To your left, the mouth of the passage is natural, hewn by time. Looking more closely, you can see carvings near the base of the opening. Talons and feathers. Beyond the threshold you see only shadows.

You realize you will have to enter one of the passages to see what is inside. But which way is the correct one?

Will you take the passage to your right, the one guarded by the mouth of the carved serpent? If so, proceed to 33.

Or, will you take the passage to your left, the one adorned with carvings of talons and feathers? If this is your chosen path, turn to 37.

31

You won't back down, you vow. You've come too far in your quest to free the king of the Citadel of Ten Thousand Pearls. You grit your teeth and wave your blade in the air.

"The carpet's mine," you hiss. "Go away. Go back to your tower and your harem girls."

The sha'ir laughs.

"Poor Jamil," he scolds. "You are so young to die."

You ready your weapon, knowing you have no choice but to fight him. You are young and nimble, and you have a powerful magic weapon in your hands.

The sha'ir keeps his distance and begins mumbling something you can't quite hear. Before you can react, the mountain begins to rumble and pebbles and rocks dance at your feet. You struggle to keep your balance and your grip on the sword.

The sha'ir laughs louder, and the rumbling increases. A hole opens up directly below your feet. For a moment you hang suspended in the air, then you plummet into blackness, and the mountain swallows you up.

THE END

32

A tale. That's it. You will make up a story. If you told her the truth, she'd likely demand a wish when you freed the king of the Citadel of Ten Thousand Pearls.

"Look, I'm in a hurry and I need to retrieve this bottle," you begin. "It belonged to my uncle, who died a few years ago. He left it to me in his will. The bottle isn't worth much, you understand. But it is all I have left to remember him by. My uncle meant an awful lot to me."

The girl pokes out her bottom lip, as if she is sympathizing with your loss, then her face wrinkles quizzically. Perhaps something in your expression is giving you away. Can she tell that you are lying? Truth is always the best course, your parents taught you. And, for the most part, you have lived by the truth.

"Are you sure it isn't valuable?" she purrs. "Are you sure this bottle tucked away in my grandfather's warehouse is not worth . . . something?"

Wonderful. She's likely as greedy as she is beautiful. It is a good thing you did not tell her the truth. She probably would have talked you out of all the wishes. No wonder her family owns such a big warehouse. They probably charge a hefty percentage for storing things here.

"You know," she begins again, leaning forward over the desk and batting her blue eyes at you. "We have the most valuable spices in all of Huzuz stored here— some are worth more per pound than gold. For me to divert my time from our precious spices to find some worthless bottle would be foolish—unless there were something in it for me."

"Fine. You'll receive a finder's fee. Help me find the bottle, and I'll reward you."

"With what?" she persists. "How much of a reward shall I receive?"

You shuffle your feet and stare at the floor. "Because the bottle has such a sentimental attachment, I will reward you with ten gold dinars."

She sits up, more alert and interested. "That does not seem so sentimental to me."

"All right, twenty dinars."

She pauses and smiles, cocking her ear toward you as if she is having a difficult time hearing you.

"Very well, forty dinars, and not a copper bit more."

"Done," she says, grinning. "Now, let me check my aunt's records and see where this bottle is stored."

You attempt to smile back, wondering where you will get the gold to meet her bribe. Ah, well, it's a minuscule portion of the treasure you will receive from the soon-to-be-freed djinni.

"Hmmm. Let's see here," she murmurs. "What did you say your dear departed uncle's name was?"

"Rashad. Rashad al-Azzazi."

A puzzled expression crosses her brow. "That name sounds familiar. Was he from Sikak, City of Coins?"

"Uh, no," you think quickly. "He's from a lot of places, though. He traveled around a great deal."

Seemingly satisfied, she goes back to the sheets of vellum. "Ah, I see a record here of goods belonging to a Sha'ir Rashad al-Azzazi. About a year ago the money he paid for storage ran out. According to our records, we sold the lot of his goods a few months ago—rather cheaply it appears—to the al-Dinak family, who runs a lesser warehouse closer to the wharf."

She offers you a sad smile. "I'm sorry, but the al-Dinaks are quick to turn a profit. I suspect they long ago sold your uncle's bottle."

Your heart sinks. You were so close. Still, you can't give up hope. You've come so far on this most unusual quest. The girl notes your disappointment and scrawls something on a blank sheet of parchment.

"Here," she offers. "Just in case they haven't sold it. These are directions to their warehouse. It's not far. Tell them Alia sent you."

"Thank you, Alia," you say, as you turn and leave the warehouse. "You have been most kind." You are disheartened that you could not find the bottle and that you lied to her about your "dead" uncle.

Turn to 55.

33

You decide to choose the path of the snake, and approaching the fork, you step inside the jaws of the serpent. The entrance is much more elaborate than the other, so perhaps more people used this path.

Your lanternlight chases some of the shadows from the walls as you step beyond the portal. The chamber beyond the mouth is pleasantly cool, refreshing you and making you forget your thirst. It is a wonder such a place exists beneath the burning sands of the desert. You remember tales in the marketplace when you were younger, stories about great underground palaces and temples hidden beneath Zakhara's desert sands. Places fashioned by caliphs and wizards and hidden from the eyes of men so the chambers could safely store their treasure. But those were stories for children.

The chamber you are in has no semblance of a palace or a temple, and despite the carved serpent's mouth, the space inside was naturally made. The walls were never mined or worked, smooth in places where water has run down them for years. A spring must be nearby—a spring or an oasis above.

Yet this chamber was home to someone decades upon decades ago. Glancing at the walls, you see paintings, most of them worn with the years. The paintings are of snakes—large ones, small ones, some of gigantic propor-tions, and others that look half man, half reptile. The images are fascinating, and they look very, very old.

What hand painted them? You study them closely. You are curious, and you have no desire to leave this comfortably cool place.

Every painting shows the snake and snake-beings traveling deeper into this cavern. Deciding that you must continue your quest before the oil in your lantern runs out, you follow their course and enter yet another chamber.

This one is immense, and your lantern's light barely reaches the walls. Even so, you can see clearly that this is where the passage stops, for there are no doors leading out from this room. Instead, ringing the room at about the height of your shoulders, you see the carved heads of serpents. The heads extend outward from the wall, as if their snake bodies are imbedded in the rock. All of the heads have their jaws open, and they all face toward the center of the room.

There must be a hundred snake heads! The snakes are carved so exquisitely they look real. Following their stony gaze, you look to the floor in the center of the room. There, on a smooth section of rock, you spy a canvas sack, large and untouched by the elements or time.

As you take in your surroundings, your thoughts are disturbed by a *plink* sound. It is quickly followed by another. And another. Whirling to find the source of the noise, you spot a gold dinar coin slide out of the mouth of one of the serpents. The one next to it also disgorges a golden dinar. The gold shimmers in your lanternlight. . . . *plink* . . . *plink*. Indeed, each of the heads is releasing golden dinars onto the floor.

Here is your chance to become rich, Jamil! You will not have to come back here with tools and your fellow pearl divers. You can grab the canvas sack and fill it with as much gold as you can carry. What do you do, young pearl diver?

Do you collect the gold? If so, turn to 35.
Or are you eager to complete your quest with no more delay? If so, go back to the other passage—the one with the carved talons and feathers, and turn to 37.

34

You can't beat the sha'ir. He is too powerful and has too much magic at his command. You are beaten. You toss the blade to the rocky ground, hold your hands at your sides, and back away.

"You win," you state simply. "Take the carpet and leave me alone."

"I'll do just that, Jamil," Sha'ir Rashad al-Azzazi calmly states as he scoops up the carpet pieces. "The weapon is yours," he adds, pointing at your magic sword. "I've no use for such barbarous things."

He motions with his fingers and disappears in a puff of gray smoke.

You are alone on the side of a mountain somewhere in the Land of Fate. You start to pick your way down the rocky slope.

It will be a very long walk home.

THE END

35

You grab the canvas sack. There is time to search for the carpet section later—*after* you are rich! You set your lantern in the center of the room and rush to one of the serpents. After scooping up handfuls of coins from the floor, you hold your sack beneath a serpent's mouth, happily watching the gold dinars plink into the canvas folds.

It is difficult to hold the sack, the gold inside is so heavy. Still, you are persistent. You grit your teeth, brace your legs, and struggle to hold on to the sack.

Plink . . . plink . . . plink . . . More gold falls into your sack. *Plink . . . plink . . . slam!*

The noise came from behind you. Glancing over your shoulder, you notice the way you came in is sealed. A great boulder has slipped into the passageway, preventing you from going back the way you came.

You carefully set down the sack, keeping the mouth of it open so more dinars can find their way inside. In another few moments it should be filled.

You circle the room, looking for another way out.

Nothing. No exit anywhere that you can see.

"Oh, no! My carpet!" you cry, noticing that the floor of the chamber is covered with gold coins—dinars that have covered up your sections of the carpet. You shift the coins, hoping to find the sections of the rug, but the coins are multiplying too quickly.

Plink . . . plink . . . plink.

The sound grows annoyingly louder until it is almost deafening. The coins spill from the serpents' mouths faster now, like water spurting out of a fountain. The entire chamber floor is covered.

Faster and faster the coins come until you are up to your knees in gold and you can barely move. Still, you can find no way out, and there seems to be no end to the riches.

Higher and higher the gold rises. Haku! Is there no end to the riches? Perhaps if the mountain of coins grows high enough you can search along the ceiling of the chamber. Perhaps there is a way out onto the desert sands above.

You struggle to stay atop the gold, climbing in the center of it, and working to free your feet from the cool metal. The coins cut the skin on your feet and hands as you rise with the coins toward the ceiling.

Carefully balancing yourself on the ever-growing mound of coins, you search along the ceiling. There has to be a way out. There has to be!

You are on your knees now. There is not enough room to stand between the coins and the ceiling. Why did you have to be so greedy? Why couldn't you have concentrated on searching for the next piece of carpet?

The mound of gold rises still, pinning you between the rocky ceiling and the coins. The air is thin. It is hard to breathe, and the gold presses you uncomfortably against the ceiling.

The gold fills the gaps between your limbs and the ceiling, swallowing you and drowning you in its metallic embrace.

THE END

36

The desert riders are your best hope, you decide. Surely they have food and water with them, and the nomads of Zakhara are known for being charitable.

You trot toward the growing cloud of sand and shout, "Over here! This way!"

The cloud moves in your direction. As it nears, you can see that four horses are responsible for stirring up the sand. They gallop toward you, their hair coated with sweat and their mouths foamy white from the heat. Seated on the lead horse is a woman! No! She is the tan djinni from the rose-colored tower in Sikak. Her purple eyes bore into you, and you realize she has been sent to get you.

You whirl on your heels and run, your feet spraying

sand behind you. Faster! you scold yourself. I must move faster.

Then, suddenly, your feet are treading on air. You are floating, and the horses come to a stop beneath you. The tan djinni dismounts and points a finger at you. The riders with her are grim-faced and coated with sand. They scowl and follow her lead, grabbing ropes from their horses' packs.

"Jamil!" the tan djinni calls. "You will come with me! My master the sha'ir wants his carpet back, and I am forced to obey."

You are slowly lowered to the ground, and the men with the djinni roughly tie you up and take the carpet sections from you. You feel yourself being lifted and tossed over the rump of a horse.

"Wh-What will happen to me?" you ask.

"The sha'ir will question you," the djinni answers flatly. "He can't afford to let you free. You know about the treasure trove, the carpet, and the king of the Citadel of Ten Thousand Pearls." She notices your worried expression. "He won't kill you," she adds, trying to comfort you. "You're young and strong. You will make a good slave. Let's move!"

The horses gallop back the way they came, kicking up sand that gets in your mouth and eyes.

You have failed Tala, the sea djinni. Now it will be the evil sha'ir who will find her husband—doubtless to coax wishes and more from the imprisoned djinni. And you will be in as bad a position as the king of the Citadel of Ten Thousand Pearls. You will find out what it is like to live as a slave.

THE END

37

This must be the way I should go, you think to yourself as you look at the passage with talons and feathers carved at the base. Looking closer at the carvings, you spot the profile of an eagle's head.

Eagle talons and feathers, you think to yourself. Why would anyone carve eagle talons under the desert? Indeed, why would anyone make a passageway look like the mouth of a serpent?

You take the path of the eagle, and step into a chamber with rough-hewn walls. Your lantern light dances eerily against the cracks and crevices, and cavorting shadows send shivers up and down your spine. Despite your momentary chill, the air inside is warm and dry, though not as uncomfortable as the air sweeping across the desert far above.

All about the chamber are paintings of eagles in flight. The paintings are old, the colors faded and muted. You move closer out of curiosity and hold the lantern so you can see the images better. The flickering light playing across the stone walls makes it look as if the painted birds are flying.

There are eagles of all sizes. Their colors are subtle, pale yellows and browns, grays with hints of black. You wonder how the artist captured their movements so realistically. But there are fantastical colors on some of the eagles as well, deep blues and orchids, reds, melon shades, and burnt oranges. Despite the age-worn paint, the creatures appear noble, and the art is so precise you imagine the artist having living creatures to copy.

You find yourself staring hypnotically at them for several moments, imagining their wings beating, feeling the air in the chamber move about you. You can hear the sound of wings, too. Or perhaps you just think you hear the wings' beatings. Perhaps it is just a trick of the cavern air. Finally, breaking away, you step back and notice that the birds on the left side of the chamber are all flying the same direction, toward a shadow-draped passageway in the distance. The birds on the right side of the chamber are flying toward it, too.

"I will follow the eagles," you whisper, stepping toward the passageway.

The darkness swallows you as you enter the corridor, for your lantern gutters and goes out. The passage is as dark as the bottom of the sea at night. You would be much happier if you could see where you were and where you were going. Shall you go back into the eagle chamber and try to make your lantern work? Turning your head, you can see nothing but blackness behind you. Or do you go forward? There is blackness there, too.

You feel the bottom of your lantern with your free hand. It is warm. Your fingers inch upward toward the wick.

"Ow!" The lantern hadn't gone out—it still burns! The wick is lit, yet there is blackness. There is magic at work, you realize, some force that was meant, perhaps, to frighten you. It is succeeding. Carefully retracing your steps, you back into the eagle chamber and the light illuminates the painted birds again. Testing your theory of the magical darkness, you thrust your lantern into the darkened passageway and plunge yourself into blackness again. You pull the lantern close to your body and stare at the painted eagles.

"Shall I go forward?" you ask yourself, staring numbly at the blackness beyond. Perhaps I can feel my way beyond the magic night and my lantern will again work. Or perhaps I will be feeling my way to my doom. Or shall I retreat and try the passageway with the snake mouth, the carved image with polished jade eyes?

If you move forward into the darkness, braving the unknown, turn to 6.

If you return to the snake passageway, turn to 33.

38

You will fly from here. The magic of the carpet is faster than your tired legs. You roll over, so that the new piece of carpet is beneath you. You sit up, yawn and rub your eyes for effect, and grab hold of the pieces of carpet. Somehow, magically, the carpet moves together, sewing itself until it is one piece.

Get me out of here now! your mind screams, and the carpet complies, lifting you up off the treasure-coated floor and carrying you from the chamber.

"Come back, trespasser!" the giant bellows.

Faster! you command, and the carpet increases its speed, somehow navigating the black corridors. Through the taloned portal it flies and out into the broad chamber where you first fell through the sand. The fragment rises, nearly traveling straight up, and you have to hold on to it with both hands to keep from falling off. Higher you climb, out the hole in the roof of the chamber and into the night sky of the desert above.

Your grin is wide and your chest filled with pride. You got the last piece of carpet without a fight!

Turn to 40.

39

You'll not tell her the truth about the bottle and the king of the Citadel of Ten Thousand Pearls. She's probably as greedy as she is pretty, and she'd want a wish or two from the freed djinni. And you'll not make up a story, either. Lying will only get you into more trouble. So you'll break the law—just a little. You'll break into the yellow warehouse after dark. With a polite smile and a bow, you apologize for taking the clerk's time and leave.

For nearly five hours you stroll about the warehouse district and the wharves, drawing curious stares from dock and warehouse workers. More than once a friendly Huzuz native asks if he could assist you, provide directions perhaps, as you seem lost. You decline, saying you are waiting for a friend. Eventually the stares stop, and the workers dismiss you as no one to worry about.

When the sunset comes, you make your way to the yellow warehouse. You discovered from casual conversation with the dock laborers that it belongs to the al-Farif family. Though the warehouse is large, it is not as immense as those it sits between.

Still, you learn from conversations with passing merchants that what is inside is valuable. The al-Farif family deals primarily in spices, some said to be more valuable per pound than gold. Of course, the workers say the family stores all manner of things, as do many of the other warehouses. In fact, the family has two other warehouses, one near the river and another in the heart of the city.

The sky grows increasingly dark, and the lights from the wharf dim as more and more workers go home. When shadows coat this section of town like paint on a new house, you circle the building, looking for a way in. The front door is too obvious. There is no back door. Odd. However, there is a window high off the ground. You can reach it by moving a few crates underneath it. Though the task should not be too difficult, you are a little nervous. After all, breaking into an underground chamber in the desert—occupied by only a construct— is one thing. Breaking into a warehouse filled with valuable spices owned by a living person is another matter entirely.

Well, Jamil, are you getting cold feet? Is it possible you don't have the heart for thievery? If you are reconsidering your actions, you could wait until the morning and go talk to the woman inside the office again. You could tell her the truth about the bottle and the djinni inside.

If you wait until morning, return to the warehouse, and tell the truth, turn to 42.

If you instead spend the night making up a lie, then return to the warehouse in the morning and tell the clerk the lie, turn to 32.

Or, if you muster the guts to climb in that window and find the bottle *tonight* so you can be a caliph *tomorrow*, continue to 51.

40

At last, you have the pieces of the carpet gathered! It was a feat and an adventure.

As you skim over the desert, you sit back and study the carpet beneath you, trying to comprehend what the silver and gold threads represent. There are no labels, nothing to indicate cities, the names of islands, the names of geographic features.

Still, parts of the map look familiar. You stare at it intently. Yes, there . . . there is where Jumlat, your home, should be, and beside it is the Golden Gulf and the islands. Ah, the map is much easier to understand now. The land is sewn in silver thread, and the water in red. There are the mountains, the rivers. You see the great desert, and judging by the stars overhead, and the map, you can tell you are right in the middle of the desert—or, rather, several hundred feet above it. You glance at the embroidered islands and guess where the one-eyed giant lived, and you rub your fingers over the tall, rocky mountains, where you got the third piece of the carpet.

The person who created this carpet was gifted with needlework, for the finest of threads show paths through hills and roads between cities.

But where are you going now? Where, decades ago, did that old sha'ir put the bottle storing the king of the Citadel of Ten Thousand Pearls? Just where is this magical carpet taking you?

The hours pass, and you doze on and off. You occupy your waking hours with thoughts of treasure and beautiful women—all things the king of the Citadel of Ten Thousand Pearls can give you once you set him free. You've heard that djinn can grant three wishes to people who free them. When you rescued Tala from the bottom of the Golden Gulf, she gave no wishes—though at the time you did not think to ask for any.

This time will be different. This time you will have your wishes ready when you open the flask—you will be prepared. The king will reward you out of gratitude, and he and his wife can go back to their Citadel of Ten Thousand Pearls. You will be free from djinn and sha'irs, and you will be rich beyond your imagination.

You lean over the edge of the carpet, studying the puffy clouds underneath you. Lights appear in cities below, and the sky there looks darker. Interesting, you think. Above the clouds it is still daylight, while below, the world is getting ready to sleep. Then you see it— you glimpse the sunset from your airborne position. Your breath is taken away, and you find yourself staring into the retreating fiery orb, which has painted the clouds myriad shades of peach, pink, yellow, and red. No more beautiful sight have you seen anywhere, and it is so majestic you forget about wishes and wealth. You only want this sight to go on forever.

You ride through the night and witness the dawning sun. It is not yet high enough to warm the sky, and you shiver. Below you is a massive city. Your eyes fly to the carpet. You are above Huzuz, City of Delights! This is said to be the most beautiful city in all the Land of Fate. For an instant, you think the carpet will fly beyond this place to another remote and inhospitable corner of the world. But then the carpet slows and gently dips toward the city.

Yes! You are going to the City of Delights, a place you always dreamed about visiting.

Perhaps in Huzuz you can find some proper clothes —after you find a way to acquire a few dinars to buy them with. You doubt a young man wandering around in an overlarge linen robe soiled with sand and dirt and blood will gain much respect in the City of Delights. You can't help but grin, thinking of the city. It is a place you'd always wanted to see, and now you will be going there, though not truly of your own volition. You will find the djinni king's bottle, explore the city, then wish him to make you a caliph.

After you find the king's bottle.

The bottle!

Where in the city could it be? The city is large. Huge.

Your heart sinks.

You slump onto the carpet and peer over the edge, dejectedly watching the world go by below you. The gleaming minarets and sparkling domes of the city only mildly lift your spirits.

"Great visitor!" you hear a voice exclaim from nowhere. You whirl around as much as you can on the flying piece of cloth, but see only the sky and clouds.

"Welcome to Huzuz, City of Delights, Heart of the Heart of Zakhara!" A ten-foot-tall figure materializes before you, hovering in the air. He is a deeply tanned bald man dressed in a finely embroidered caftan and ornate silk slippers. "I am the djinni imam, purveyor of information, regaler of stories, orator of legends, and most knowledgeable guide for Huzuz, City of Delights."

The djinni grins broadly, revealing impossibly white, even teeth. He throws back his head and laughs heartily. "And you are . . . ?"

"Jamil," you state, staring blankly at him.

"Jamil, then," the djinni replies. "Move over Jamil, so that I might do my job and entertain you with details of the city."

Numbly, you move over so the djinni can join you on the carpet. His form seems to grow smaller until he is roughly your size, then he sits cross-legged on the front of the carpet and points at the city below.

"Behold Golden Huzuz, City of Delights, home to the Palace of the Enlightened Throne where lives the Grand Caliph, who dines on the finest foods and wines imported from the Far East," the djinni recites on and on.

While many of the buildings below you look no different than those in Jumlat, City of Multitudes, there are also palaces and minarets and domes of remarkable splendor. You fly over low, flat buildings, likely homes to the poor; small domed buildings with courtyards filled with flowers and exotic plants; suqs, modest markets; mosques with colorful tiled roofs; and constructions of foreign design with half-moon-shaped roofs of brilliant reds and greens.

"Jamil, are you listening to me?"

"Huh? Uh, yes, djinni imam," you stammer. "I'm enjoying the tour."

"Behold the great buildings of the city, the palaces of caliphs and wealthy merchants. Many of the minarets are decorated with inlaid metals, the purest gold and silver that can be found. Inside these grand structures are paintings that are the most beautiful in all of Zakhara. Powerful people live in these buildings that stretch to the sky, Jamil.

"And over there are the universities."

"Universities? Schools?"

"Yes, Jamil. Did not you go to school?"

You glower at him. Yes, you went to school. But you never had the opportunity to attend for several years in a row or to study at a university. You remember your fellow pearl divers gossiping about going to the City of Delights to study the sea and more at the famed universities. Idle talk.

"Yes, I went to school," you answer with an edge to your voice.

"Anyone in Golden Huzuz can attend schools, and anyone with the proper amount of gold dinars is allowed into the universities. Even beggars save their scant earnings to attend classes. They say more than twenty thousand students attend the university. I had considered teaching there, magic courses you understand. But . . . let us say I had reasons to pursue this career."

"What reasons?"

It was the djinni's turn to glower. "The Grand Caliph has ordered me to guide newcomers about the city. He was . . . displeased . . . with my service to him."

You stop yourself from asking more questions.

"Enough of the schools. Let us look to the river. Below is the Al-Sarif River, which, years ago, was Golden Huzuz's northern border. But as the city grew, it sprawled across the river. See the two djinn far below pushing that ferry across the river? They take people back and forth between the sections of the city."

"Did they anger the caliph, too?"

The djinni ignores your question and points to

another section of the city. "There is the clothier's district—a place you should visit, young Jamil. And there, the caravan district. Beyond is the Grand Bazaar, the most important and largest bazaar in all of Zakhara."

You peer over the edge of the carpet and find yourself agreeing with the djinni. Entire cities could fit on the land the bazaar occupies. There are permanent buildings, tents, stalls with brightly colored awnings and flags, vendors with pushcarts, and more. Though you are still high above the sites, you imagine the singing, the haggling, the smell of fresh-baked bread.

"You wish to stop there, Jamil?"

You quickly nod your head, then scowl. "No. Not today."

The djinni furrows his brow, but continues the tour.

"There is the court district, the house of al-Thuria, and the Gate of the Ghost. Look you at the pilgrim's district and the grand mosques that attract the faithful from all parts of our country. See the Mosque of Brave Hajama, god of the fearless. There are lions guarding the worshipers' section. And look at the Mosque of Kor the Old and the Mosque of Zann the Wise—he whose followers are said to be among the brightest and most perceptive of all those in Golden Huzuz. And there is the Golden Mosque."

Truly, you have never seen such a grand building. From the tales you know, it is not a place where worshippers of one god go, but a place open to all those who pray to Zakhara's enlightened gods. The pillars and dome are laced with gold that sparkles in the morning sun. Sitting on a mound of sculptured earth adorned with trimmed bushes and plants, the mosque's minarets rise taller than any building in the golden city.

"Three hundred feet those minarets reach, touching the clouds that dance over Huzuz, City of Delights. We must be careful not to fly over the minarets. It is against the law to be so disrespectful. Neither can we fly over the Grand Caliph's palace. Now, let us be away to the harbor." With a flick of his index finger, the djinni changes the course of the carpet, angling it toward the sea.

"Nowhere else in Zakhara is the water so beautiful, so clear and clean. The fish that swim in the waters are the largest and tastiest and swim willingly into the fishermen's nets," the djinni brags. "Here is the harbor district, where people such as yourself can find places to stay for only a few copper bits."

"People such as myself!"

"Jamil, do not be ashamed that you are poor," the djinni scolds, looking at your bedraggled attire and mottled carpet.

"Poor?!"

"Why yes. It is obvious from the way you talk and the way you dress—and from this worn carpet—that you have little money."

You bluster at the impudent djinni. "I'm not *that* poor. Besides, I'll be rich soon—very soon I might add. Richer than you can imagine."

The djinni raises his eyebrows. "Coming into some great inheritance, are you?"

"No. I'm going to rescue a sea djinni, and he will reward me for all of my efforts."

The djinni throws back his head and laughs. He doesn't believe you! Well, all the better. You point to the section of town below to change the subject.

"Why are there so many people below us?" you ask, getting the djinni to stop laughing.

"The harbor is busy—always. Ships come in at all hours to disgorge pearls from Jumlat and other less fortunate cities and unload the fine goods Golden Huzuz will sell in her marketplaces. On occasion, the harbor has been known to host ships from the wretched barbarian countries far, far to the north. And, just once, I saw a great sailing ship float into the harbor from the sky. Now, over here is the Grand Caliph's harbor. See his barge— there it is, just twist your head a little. Is it not the grandest ship you have looked upon? And beyond is the trade harbor filled with the finest galleys in Zakhara, and dotted with huge ships from other lands."

The carpet continues its journey, and you find your-self caught up in the splendor and wonder of the City of Delights. Perhaps the djinni is right: there is no greater city in all of Zakhara. The carpet angles back toward the heart of the city, and you pass over massive buildings. The carpet falters for a moment, beginning to dive toward a large yellow building, but the djinni guide waggles his fingers and the carpet rises again.

That's it! your mind screams. The carpet was trying to take you to the king's bottle.

"Djinni! Where are we? What is below us? That building?"

"A warehouse." The djinni wrinkles his nose. "This, Jamil, is the warehouse district. A necessary part of the city's operation, for the buildings house goods going in and out of the city and store merchandise for sellers in the Grand Bazaar and elsewhere. Even the Grand Caliph has warehouses."

"We have to go down there."

"Why ever would you want to be in the warehouse district when there are so many wonderful places to explore in Golden Huzuz?"

"I'll explore them later," you state. "Now make this carpet land."

"You are a most unusual tourist, Jamil."

"I'm not a . . . never mind."

The carpet lands outside the largest warehouse, a yellow structure with fresh white trim. You have a feel-ing you are in the right place; it was over this building that the carpet started to descend. You had feared you would be weeks or months in the city—perhaps a year—exploring nooks and crannies in search of a bot-tle with a fluted neck.

"My payment, please."

"What?!"

"My payment for the tour." The djinni begins to grow, stopping at his ten-foot-tall stature. "I am always paid when I guide visitors around the city. And you said you are not poor."

"I did not ask you to guide me anywhere."

"But you did not turn me away," the djinni huffs. "That is the same thing as asking me to guide you."

"I don't have any coins," you sputter.

"But you have a flying rug. That would be adequate payment."

"I need the rug."

The djinni wrinkles his brow and grows another foot taller. The passersby pay no attention.

"I need the rug to help me find something."

"I'd say you need the rug to help you come up with my payment."

"Listen," you start, your mind creating a tale. No use telling him about the bottle. "I need this rug so I can sell it and purchase clothes and a cutlass. I can't keep walking around with this dirty robe and a little knife."

The djinni waves his hand and you find yourself wearing an embroidered caftan, not unlike his own, though not as ostentatious. At your side is a cutlass, like the one you found in the cave, but without the glow of magic.

"There! You have clothes and a sword, and I will have the rug."

Well, Jamil, it looks like you have a dilemma to face. Do you give the djinni the carpet and hope to find the bottle in the warehouse on your own—provided the yellow warehouse is indeed the right place? You are resourceful, Jamil. You know what Tala's bottle looked like. Perhaps her husband's looks the same. Or, you can refuse the djinni. But if you upset him, who knows what he'll do?

Do you give the djinni the carpet? If so, turn to 52.

Or, do refuse to pay him, knowing you'd be lost without the carpet? If so, flip to 45.

41

You cannot take the boy with you. It would be too dangerous—especially with someone else in Golden

Huzuz looking for the bottle. You have your suspicions that it is the young Sha'ir Rashad al-Azzazi or one of his agents.

You bid the boy farewell, thank him for his help, and step out into the street. The City of Delights is so alive and vibrant. The streets are filled with people from all walks of life.

You stride through the Grand Bazaar, finding it difficult to keep your mind on your task. The scents and sounds compete for your attention. To your right are rug dealers, and to your left a barber shop. Ahead are stalls offering pastries, sculptures, weapons, jewelry, clothes, and more.

Would that you had dinars to browse! Shaking your head to clear your thoughts, you concentrate on finding the palace. "Once I have freed the king of the Citadel of Ten Thousand Pearls, I can have anything in this market-place I desire," you whisper. "The king will certainly be so very happy to be free that he will grant any wish."

Your thoughts drift away from wealth for a moment when you spy a glass merchant with plates and goblets and multicolored flasks. What would it be like to be trapped in a bottle for decades, not able to go anywhere or see any of the marvels Zakhara has to offer? You feel sorry for the king and increase your pace.

"Hey, watch where you're going!" a surly man shouts as he pushes you out of his way.

Paying more attention to where you are walking, you resume your course to the center of Golden Huzuz. From your tour with the djinni, you remember the palace being near the middle—and occupying a considerable amount of land.

Suddenly a shiver races up your spine, and you look about the marketplace. You have an odd feeling, as if someone were watching you, following you. But there are so many people about that you cannot spot the watcher. Perhaps it is the youth from the warehouse who wanted to come with you. You don't need a boy slowing you down. Looking through the crowd you spot several children, but the one from the warehouse is not among them.

Still, the odd feeling persists. You take another pass through the crowd, and your eyes come to rest on a cloaked figure clinging to the shadows under a marketplace vendor's awning. The man's shape looks familiar. A group of young women pass between you and the man; they snicker and gossip and point at the goods on display. You sprint to look beyond them, only to discover that the man has disappeared.

Perhaps it is nothing. Perhaps the man was simply another shopper and was not watching you at all. Still, you quicken your stride and move through the Grand Bazaar.

You pass near mosques and cut through the pilgrims' district, where the devout come to find enlightenment. You wonder if you are enlightened, and consider just what enlightenment might mean. You see the Mosque of Kor the Old, the god of wisdom. Several elderly men gather outside the front door. You know age is respected and honored among the worshipers of Kor. Beyond is the Mosque of Free Haku, the only building of worship without a dome. Perhaps you can visit this place after you have the bottle.

Your feet are tired and sore by the time you make your way to the court district, where the buildings are impressive, though not as beautiful as the mosques. You turn a corner, and your mouth drops open in wonder. During your bird's-eye tour, you had believed the Palace of the Enlightened Throne was impressive. But on the ground it looks even more so. The thing is virtually a city within a city, with a gold-decorated gate surrounding the whole affair.

How are you going to find your way inside and locate a fluted blue bottle? It could take you weeks to search through all of the rooms inside—and that is providing you don't get caught and thrown in jail.

You stand back from the gates and watch groups of people moving inside under the careful eyes of guards. You could slip in with them, moving like you have business to conduct inside. The embroidered caftan the djinni guide gave you makes you look presentable. Or, you could go back to the warehouse and seek the help of the young boy, though you are not certain that he would have a better means to get inside. It is time to make a decision, Jamil.

Do you lose yourself in a group of people passing through the palace gate? If so, turn to 53.

Or, do you return to the al-Dinak warehouse and ask the boy to guide you? If so, turn to 56.

42

You look into her gorgeous eyes and tell her everything—about your life as a pearl diver, about finding the bottle on the sunken ship and freeing the djinni inside, and about Tala coaxing you to find her husband, the king of the Citadel of Ten Thousand Pearls. You leave out few details, as you believe that if you are honest with this young woman, she will help you.

"Now do you understand why I must have this bottle?" you gasp, winded from your long explanation. "In fact, you can keep the bottle. Just let me open it and free the king."

She frowns, her face lovely even wearing that expression. "He has been in a glass bottle for decades?"

You nod solemnly.

"You are certainly a brave and sympathetic man to risk so much to come here and free a djinni you do not know. He will be most grateful to you. And he'll probably grant you wishes."

Here it comes, you realize as her eyes sparkle. She puts down the quill, strokes her cheek, and glances about the dingy office.

"Such a kind man as yourself would share a wish, I think, with a beautiful girl who helped him."

Resigned, you nod. "All right. You can have one wish. *One.* I've taken a lot of chances and nearly gotten myself killed coming this far. The one-eyed giant, the evil sha'ir, the metal construct. I'm going to get something out of this."

She grins and leaps to her slippered feet. "Oh, one wish! I shall be rich! Hmmm. What is your name?"

"Jamil," you state quietly. "Jamil the Gullible," you moan even more quietly.

She quickly locks the front door and pulls a shade to indicate the warehouse is closed. Grabbing your hand, she tugs you into the warehouse, where the scents of spices are even stronger.

"My grandfather owns this warehouse," she gushes. "He has the most expensive and best spices anywhere in Golden Huzuz. In fact, they are the best in all of Zakhara. He claims if a spice exists, it has passed through this warehouse. He also has warehouses near the river and a small one in the middle of the city."

You listen to her drone on about her family and the value of the goods inside this building as warehouse workers move to get out of her way. She points to bottles filled with a dark green spice and brags that a pound of that herb is worth three times a pound of gold. You are dizzy from the combination of smells by the time your path takes you to a wooden door in the back of the warehouse.

"All of the goods that are not spices are kept inside," she squeals, tugging on the latch three times before the door finally yields. She rushes inside, pulling you behind her.

You sneeze, but not from the scent of spices. A coating of fine dust covers everything inside.

"My aunt hasn't been in here for quite a while. Truly our business is spices. And these things have gone unclaimed for so long that I suspect she does not even know what is here."

You nod your head and begin searching about a room that is even smaller than the office. There are wooden boxes and ceramic flasks, canvas sacks, stacks of pelts, tanned skins, a few bolts of dust-permeated wool, and a barrel full of charcoal. From each item dangles a tag.

You brush the dust off one of the tags to read:

"Hakim al-Danifi, unpolished agate, received by Muta al-Farif." The date is eight years ago.

You sneeze. "If only I still had my carpet. This would be easy." You sort through a few of the canvas sacks, and then move them aside to see what is stored behind them. "We're looking for a flask, a blue fluted one. The tag on it should read "Rashad al-Azzazi."

"What?" the girl fumes. She pokes her finger at your arm, then puts her hands on her hips and glares at you. "Look at me, Jamil the Gullible! I am filthy. My new robe is coated with dust. You knew the name of the man who owns the bottle and yet you made me paw through this dirt?"

You look at her quizzically and note that a spider-web clings like a second veil to her hair. Though you suspect you look no better, you have encountered far worse than dust and dirt in your efforts to retrieve the carpet and the bottle.

"You did this on purpose! You wanted me to get dirty! Well, Jamil the Gullible, it looks like I was the gullible one here. My price has just gone up. I will get two of the three wishes now."

She storms from the small room, glancing back over her shoulder and calling for you to come along. Again, the warehouse workers jump out of her way, and for a moment you wonder if it would have been easier to slip into this place after dark.

Back in the small office, she sits at the desk and rifles through the vellum on top. Huffing, she searches through the desk drawers until she finds a scroll tube with a lengthy scrawled label on it. Before you can read what the tag says, she pops open the tube, pulls out a weathered piece of parchment, and begins reading, mumbling to herself as she goes.

"Wonderful. Oh this has been a truly delightful day, Jamil the Gullible. Had you told me in the beginning the name of the man who owned the bottle I wouldn't look like this, and I wouldn't be kicking you out of this office."

"What?" You stare at her incredulously. You have no intention of letting her get the bottle herself—and all three wishes the freed king of the Citadel of Ten Thousand Pearls will certainly provide. "Woman, you are not stealing the djinni out from under me!"

Her lip curls back in a snarl, and you decide she isn't so beautiful after all. "The bottle isn't here. In fact, nothing stored by Sha'ir Rashad al-Azzazi is here." She fumes and places her hands on her hips.

"Apparently the sha'ir *had* stored things with us," she sputters. "But a little more than a year ago the money he had paid for that storage ran out. My family sold the lot of his goods, including a blue fluted bottle, to the al-Dinak family. They run a shoddy warehouse closer to the wharf, and I'm positive they've sold off all the junk by now."

"No!"

The woman tilts her chin and titters. "You will never find your precious djinni now, Jamil the Gullible. Forever will the king of the Citadel of Ten Thousand Pearls rot in the bottle."

You'll not give up yet, you vow. You have come too far. "Where is the al-Dinak warehouse? Will you at least tell me how to get there?"

"My pleasure, Jamil the Gullible," she coos, rattling off directions and pointing her finger at the door. "Now I must clean myself. Be off!"

Turn to 55.

43

You are drawn to the door of cherrywood, where the rocs fly above the desert. You saw one such roc of giant proportions but a day or two ago. You were in the desert, and fortunately you did not fall prey to the great creature's claws.

Opening the polished silver latch, you step inside and gasp as the heat takes your breath away. You stand on sand; the floor of the room is coated in it, just like a desert dune. The air is dry and warm, though not as hot as the desert. High above, you see clouds and something whirling in them, a miniature sandstorm perhaps. All along the walls are pictures of desert scenes, expertly done. They look so real.

The faces of the people painted on the wall are wrinkled from the sun, their eyes bright, and their expressions thoughtful.

"Come closer," a voice seems to say. "Come closer and let me teach you of the desert. That's right, my friend. Step near my tent."

You pad over the sand toward the painted red and white tent, and for a moment you see its flag flying in the desert breeze. You feel the breeze, too; it whips across the ground, stirring up sand and forcing you to blink.

"Quickly, young man! We must be on our horses, for the great djinni draws near!"

"What?" Whirling, you see a man motioning to you, one of the figures painted on the wall. But he is standing, moving, as are the other people you thought were but works of art. In fact, all semblance of the room is gone, replaced by a desert. You smell the meat roasting on a fire, see the juicy dates on a ceramic plate, and you hear the whinnying of the horses tied near the tent—horses that were not in the painting. You are in the painting on the wall! This room is magical!

"I said, the great djinni comes! He will whisk us far from the oasis and deposit us in the Golden Gulf for spite! The treasure will never be ours!"

"Treasure? Oasis? Where are we?"

"Are you daft, man? We are miles from the river, and only a few miles from the oasis. We must ride. The djinni must not catch us!" The man and his companions dash to their horses. You notice there is one extra horse. Yours?

You rush to catch up and grab the reigns of the horse. You struggle to get on the beast, a much different task than climbing aboard a camel, which kneels for you. One of the men reaches down and pulls you up by your flowing white robe.

Robe? What happened to the caftan the djinni gave

you? The men dig their heels into the sides of the horses and off they ride, to the northwest, you guess, judging by the position of the sun. You follow, urging your mount along. The horse moves fast, its hooves flying across the white sands of the desert and into the warm breeze.

"Hurry, he is gaining!" one of the men shouts.

Behind you, another wind picks up, this one stronger and hotter, and definitely not natural. The ground shakes, and sand erupts everywhere.

"No! He is upon us. The great djinni is upon us! Haku preserve us all!"

Glancing over your shoulder and nearly knocking from your head a turban you did not realize you wore, you spot a massive figure: a djinni at least twenty feet tall with shoulders as wide as your horse from nose to tail. He rises from the sand, a whirlwind whipping about him. He opens his mouth and laughs, deep and long.

"Desert fleas!" his voice bellows across the sand. "I have caught you, and now you are mine!"

He laughs again, and you and the other men spur your horses faster and faster. He rides the sand behind you like an insect skating across the placid water of Jumlat's bay. You can feel his hot breath on the back of your neck.

"You are mine!" he howls.

And you feel his hand reach out and grab you about the waist.

Then the wind stops, and the howling laughter of the djinni ends. Your robes are gone; your turban is gone. You stand in a sandy-floored room in your embroidered caftan. The paintings are there, as flawless as before the djinni appeared. Looking above, you see the blue sky, but the whirlwind or sandstorm, or whatever it was, is gone, too.

Were you really in a desert, or were you dreaming?

Shrugging your shoulders and rubbing the sand from your eyes, you turn and leave the room.

If you go to the oak door, turn to 49.

If, instead, you venture to the door made of walnut, turn to 57.

44

Yes! What a wonderful idea to take some of this treasure and run! You have spied a few especially valuable-looking baubles, including the topaz the size of your fist. They're grouped nicely together, and not too far from where you lie. Even one of these pieces will be enough to hire a band of nomads. You will use part of this treasure to hire fighters to help you obtain the carpet section you seek.

You bound to your feet and sprint up a pile of gold to the topaz. The astonished construct opens its mouth in surprise. You quickly palm the gem and scoop up a pair of emerald necklaces. Whirling around, you dash straight toward the darkened passageway that brought you here. In a half-dozen strides, you are inside the comforting pitch darkness. Slowing your pace, you run your elbow alongside the cavern wall so you can retrace your steps.

Once outside it should not be too difficult to find the nomads. They can have one of the necklaces. You will keep the rest for yourself.

Emerging from the darkness, you are shocked to see the treasure chamber again. Where is the cave with the eagle paintings? How did you get back here?

Worse, standing right in front of you is the bronze construct.

"Little thief," the guardian booms. "You were foolish to steal from my master."

"Your master's dead!" you protest as he grabs you about the waist and picks you up until you are eye-to-eye with him.

"Put me down!" you demand. "Here, you can have the jewelry."

"You should not have taken the sha'ir's treasure,"

the giant drones. "My orders are clear."

You feel his fists tighten about your waist, and the wind rushes from your lungs. He slowly squeezes until the last breath of life flees from you, and your body falls limp to join the coins on the floor.

THE END

45

"Surely you are joking!" you exclaim. "You can't have my carpet! I told you I was not looking for a guide. I didn't ask you to guide me. And I most certainly have no intention of paying you. Now, begone! Find some other visitor to leech gold dinars from."

You are angry. You have no time to waste on an uninvited, pesky djinni. To stress your point, you turn your back on the creature, squat, and roll up your carpet.

"Jamil," the djinni says evenly, "you are wronging me. I am not allowed to harm others. The Grand Caliph would have my head for that. But I am not prevented from seeking compensation for my services. I hope you can swim, Jamil."

You don't hear the djinni leave, nor do you feel the ground beneath your feet give way. Yet both things happen. You gasp for air as the warm waters of Huzuz Bay close about you. The djinni transported you into the harbor and stole your carpet! How could he? Didn't he realize you could not give up the flying carpet? Well, on second or third thought, perhaps you should have simply given it to him.

It is difficult to swim in your new fancy robe; the fabric clings to your arms and legs like seaweed and makes it hard to stay afloat. You hold your breath and struggle with the garment to pull it off. The fishes swim away frantically, scared by your erratic movements. However, a large turtle pokes its head up about a yard away. It regards you with its big pool-like eyes, then dips below the surface.

"In the harbor!" you hear someone cry. "A man is drowning!"

I'm not drowning, you muse. I'm fuming. Fuming mad at a stupid djinni.

By the time you get the robe off, you feel a pair of hands lift you into a small boat. Squirming in their grasp, you reach over the side of the boat and grab your caftan before it sinks. No use losing everything to the djinni guide.

"Are you all right?" the helpful sailor asks. He feels your arms and legs and pokes at your chest to make sure you are not hurt.

"Fine," you grimace. "I had a little accident."

"Fall off your ship?"

"No. I fell afoul of a djinni," you reply, finding no reason to lie to this helpful man.

He laughs and slaps you on the back. "There are plenty of djinn in Huzuz. Take care not to anger any more of them."

The small boat eases up to the docks, and the man helps you out. The smells of the harbor assail you, reminding you of Jumlat's port. The air is filled with the scent of freshly caught fish. It is not unpleasant, and it is not unlike home. Workers scurry about the planks, unloading and loading cargo on ships of many different sizes and from many different places. This is only a part of Huzuz's harbor, and it is busier than all of Jumlat's harbor on the most active day.

"Haku, curse that djinni," you mutter as you struggle into your wet caftan. "Now how will I find that bottle?"

You scurry away from the docks, your embroidered robe dripping rivulets of sea water on the ground in your wake. Well, Jamil, you have yet another decision to make.

Do you try to find the djinni who stole the carpet? You might need it to find the king's bottle. If this is what you do, turn to 50.

Or, do you retrace your steps to the large yellow

warehouse, where you suspect the bottle might be? If
so, go to 54.

46

Well, the singing in the courtyard is grand, and the
shrubs and trees wonderful to look at, but you are
much more interested in finding the blue bottle and
leaving behind all of the people in this palatial park.
Doubtless there are hundreds of rooms to search
within the palace walls. But you are confident that you
can find the marid. After all, you have made it this far.
Fate is surely shining on you this day. Indeed, perhaps
Fate is helping you along.

You dart through a doorway in the southern end of
the courtyard, stepping between chiseled marble pillars that support a marble roof. The floor inside, also
made of marble, feels cool and smooth on your feet.

The room beyond is featureless, save for a small
fountain that bubbles and gurgles merrily. There are
many doorways off this chamber. You rub your chin
and twirl around. Well, time to begin your search. You
hope you do not get lost or accidently discover the
Grand Caliph's harem. Intruding on a palace's harem
girls, you've heard, is a crime punishable by death.

Picking a doorway, you step through to discover a
woman smoothing bolts of cloth. No doubt these were
recently purchased from merchants. She looks up and
smiles. "May I be of help? You look new to the palace."

She is clearly not a slave, as she wears a veil edged
in tiny pearls. Her clothes are too fine and her hands
are smooth, not callused from hard work. Thinking
quickly, you return her smile.

"Yes, I am new to the palace. This is my first day of
work."

She finishes smoothing the fabric and continues
speaking while she rolls up the bolt of cloth. "The buyers did well today, did they not? These will make wondrous caftans. Don't you agree?"

You nod.

"You will enjoy your time here. The Defender of the Faithful and Master of the Enlightened Throne is most pleasant to work for. No greater caliph graces the soil and sand of Zakhara. No greater man walks in the City of Delights."

"Yes, the Grand Caliph is truly great," you reply.

"What is your skill, then? What has he hired you for? You seem lost. Perhaps I can direct you." She smiles warmly at you. "The palace is large. It took me weeks to learn my way around."

Praise Haku! She is offering to guide you! She believes you are here to work. Although lying to others is something you find distasteful, telling someone you are here to steal a bottle from the Grand Caliph is a truth that could land you in jail. You think quickly. This story must be good, one that will get you close to where the bottle might be.

"I am a glass blower," you announce proudly. You place your hands in front of your mouth, mimicking the movements of the glass blowers you have seen in Jumlat's marketplace. "I am the best at my trade. My works decorate palaces throughout Zakhara. Why, some of my greatest efforts are in minarets in the City of Multitudes along the Pearl Coast. Now my work will adorn the Palace of the Enlightened Throne of the Grand Caliph."

"How remarkable!" the woman exclaims. Finished with her task, she places the bolts together and points toward the courtyard. "The Grand Caliph is on his dais, listening to the singing barber. I was listening earlier. I enjoy the music, but I have heard those tunes so many times. Do you wish to wait for the caliph, or shall I escort you through the palace? He could be a time, as he so relishes the barber's voice."

"I would not think to bother the Master of the Enlightened Throne," you reply, recalling her name for the Grand Caliph. "However, I would enjoy your company inside these palace walls. Please, to understand the Enlightened One's tastes in fine glass, I must see all that he now has. Only by looking at what he has can I create works to complement them, works that will make him happy."

She furrows her brow in contemplation. "He has so many things made of glass. I'm not sure where to start. Vases? Goblets? Sculptures perhaps? I am especially fond of his collection of glass griffins." She motions you to follow her through another doorway, and you comply. "Plates and platters? Lamps? Tables? He has a glass table the color of the dawn sky. It came all the way from L'tiraf, City of Confessions. When goblets matching the color of the table are placed upon it, guests have said the entire scene looks as if it were shaped from one piece of glass."

You listen to her rattle on and on about all of the Grand Caliph's glass treasures. She would likely show you all of them, provided no one discovered your ruse. Not only would you be in trouble in that event, you could cost this woman her job, or worse. Better not to involve her too deeply in your mission, you decide.

"I would like to look at the simple pieces first," you state. "In simplicity lies much loveliness. And from simple things come more complex creations." You are proud of your banter. "So we will start with simple creations of glass—vases, plates, and bottles. Yes, I think I would like to start by looking at the Grand Caliph's bottles."

"This way, then, kind glassblower," the woman instructs.

Through marble hallway after marble hallway you walk, passing elaborate tapestries of embroidered djinn and princes on flying carpets. One tapestry shows a djinni standing at the front of a carpet, with clouds above and below it. The djinni's face is familiar. Yes, he is the one who guided you around the City of Delights, the one who took your carpet as payment for the tour. The woman notices you staring at the djinni's image.

"You've seen him before, yes?"

"Yes," you answer. "I saw him steal a magic rug from a young man yesterday. The man did not want to part with the carpet, but the djinni took it anyway."

"He was once a friend of the Grand Caliph," the woman continues, a scowl touching her smooth face. "But the djinni stole fourteen pearls from a visiting wise man and refused to give them back. My husband became angry and ordered the djinni to serve the city for as many years as pearls he stole. I will speak to my husband of the djinni's recent theft."

"Your husband?"

"Yes, I am the fourth wife of the Grand Caliph."

Instinctively you bow to her. "I did not realize your station."

She titters, a soft, high-pitched giggle. "That is because I tire of the guards. They cannot guard me if I order them not to. Besides, there are so many guards and djinn about that I am safe here. Now, about those bottles and vases . . ."

Your path takes you through room after room filled with opulent furniture imported from the far reaches of Zakhara. Servants, visitors, guards, and others pay you no heed in the company of the fourth wife of the Grand Caliph of the Enlightened Throne. Only once does she hesitate in her course, and that is to look over her shoulder.

"For a moment I thought we were being watched," she whispers. "But that is such a silly thought. Someone is always watching me inside the palace."

Not such a silly thought, you think, remembering back to the Grand Bazaar when you caught a glimpse of the sha'ir spying on you. Could he have found his way inside the palace? No. There are too many guards. But, you reconsider, you found your way inside these marble gates with little effort.

"Here!" she announces, pulling open a carved walnut door nearly ten feet high. "Straight past this chamber is the glassware. Do not stray, or you could get lost. Wait a moment. Did you hear someone call for me?" She pauses and tilts her head. "Yes. My husband calls. I must be away. Enjoy the palace, glassblower. We shall meet again soon."

Wonderful, you think. What if she mentions to her

husband about seeing you? You suspect the Grand Caliph would remember if he hired a glassblower. You will be undone soon if she talks—and that is likely, you suspect. She hardly shut up while she was in your presence. Better be quick about this, then. Find the bottle, free the king of the Citadel of Ten Thousand Pearls, become as rich as the Grand Caliph himself!

You race through the room before you, hardly noticing the impressive surroundings. Just beyond this room, you heard her say. Just beyond here should be the Grand Caliph's bottles. You hope one is blue and fluted. But you quickly discover that "just beyond this room" amounts to a hallway of polished pink marble with black and gold veins. Floor, ceiling, and walls are made of the material, which is pleasing to the touch. The walls are decorated with sconces holding golden lamps filled with perfumed oil. The scent is musky and strong. Between the sconces, at precise, measured intervals are paintings of handsome-looking men, all similar in appearance. These are likely paintings of the caliph's relatives or ancestors, you muse. Well, no time to study them, it is time to be about your task. There are three doors off the hallway, each made of a different type of wood and each carved and polished.

One is oak and covered with the image of desert djinn in midflight. This is the door directly in front of you. The next door is rich cherrywood, its rosy surface displaying great birds, perhaps rocs, flying over the desert below. The farthest door is walnut, dark and rich-looking and decorated with the carvings of genies twirling in the sky.

The fourth wife of the Grand Caliph indicated the bottles were nearby, but behind which door?

If you open the oak door, turn to 49.

If you instead step through the cherrywood door, turn to 43.

Or, if you prefer the door made of walnut, turn to 57.

47

You lay your head back down, determined to come up with a better plan. It would be folly to try to steal some of this treasure. The construct is large and apparently made of metal. It is doubtful you could hurt it—not with your fists anyway. You suspect if you ran, it would be able to catch you in but a few steps. There has to be a better way. There has to be. But what?

You are uncomfortable, the air in the chamber is chilly. You shiver as your mind plays over the possibilities.

"Are you cold?" the giant asks emotionlessly.

"A little," you reply, not lifting your head. You wonder if it can feel anything—heat, cold, moisture, pain. It would be a sorry existence to feel nothing. But it would be nice not to be so cold. You shiver again and feel something being draped over you.

"This will make you more comfortable, young trespasser," the giant says. "Sleep well and quickly so you can leave this place."

Opening an eye to see what he placed atop you, your heart nearly stops in astonishment. The giant has placed the piece of carpet you seek over you as a blanket!

Now what do I do? you think. I gained the carpet without trying, but how do I get it out of here? I can't just lie here with my prize on top of me.

Do you jump to your feet and rush out of the chamber, toting the carpet along? If so, turn to 65.

Or do you roll atop the rug and hope it takes you and the other three pieces out of this place? If so, flip to 38.

48

"All right, my young friend," you say, trying to sound happy. "Please take me to the Grand Caliph's."

You step out into streets filled with people from all

walks of life: humans, dwarves, gnomes, and others
from exotic, far away places. The sights and sounds are
intoxicating as you and the boy move between the
buildings and along the bustling streets. You pass into
the Grand Bazaar and are assailed with the scents of
fruit and spiced meat. You wish your pearl-diving
friends could see this place.

"Do you know that my city is the best in all of
Zakhara? No city rivals the City of Delights!" the youth
babbles. "There, that is the place of the singing barber—
Gorar al-Aksar. He is the most famous man in all of the
Grand Bazaar. He does not need to cut hair or shave
faces to earn his dinars. His voice is so beautiful that the
Grand Caliph asks him to sing at the palace each week.
In fact, the barber will sing for the caliph today. That is
why he is closing up shop now. It is said he earns more
dinars singing one day for the Grand Caliph than he
makes in three months working his shop.

"And look over there. See Hakim's business? He
claims to sell clothes only to the enlightened. But he
really sells to anyone with enough copper bits and gold
dinars in their pockets. And there is my friend Janci.
He sells camels—the finest camels in all of Zakhara.
The City of Delights has the finest of everything. Do
you want to buy a camel? I know how to ride them,
and I will make sure Janci gives you a good price. I
could teach you how to ride a camel."

You shake your head and look about the marketplace. You have an odd feeling. Like someone is watching you. Someone very near. The hair prickles on the
back of your neck, and you feel uneasy. But there are so
many people about that you cannot spot the watcher.

"Did you know that Golden Huzuz was nothing
more than a small village only six hundred years ago?
That is a long time, but not so long for such a city."

The boy continues to ramble, going on about how
Golden Huzuz and all of its beautiful minarets and
domes came into being. You hear only half of what he
says, concerned about the nagging feeling of being
watched and curious about this barber who sings for

the caliph.

Then something catches your eye. A figure near a shadow-draped alley. You stop and stare, and the youth continues to babble on. At first the figure is hard to make out, then it steps away from the shadows and you recognize—Ubar! What is your pearl-diving friend Ubar doing here?

"Stay here, boy," you instruct the chattering youth. "I'll be right back."

You weave your way through the throng of busy Huzuz shoppers and dash to Ubar. He smiles a greeting and steps into the alley.

"Ubar?"

"*Psst.* In here, Jamil. I have a secret to tell you."

You follow him into the alley, a dozen questions dancing on your lips. You are glad to see your friend, but you are puzzled how he got here, so far from Jumlat on the Golden Gulf. Hmm, perhaps Tala the sea djinni has given up on you and chosen another champion. But Ubar?

"How did you get here?" you blurt.

"I followed you," Ubar replies in a hushed voice.

"Followed me? How?"

"The sha'ir," Ubar answers, his voice deepening. Your friend stands taller now—several inches taller than you remember him being, and he continues his tale. "The sha'ir bid me to follow you. He bid me to pick an image from your mind that you would be comfortable with and that would lure you away from the crowds. He bid me to kill you so you would not get the bottle. The bottle is for the young sha'ir Rashad al-Azzazi alone."

"No!" you bellow. "You are not Ubar! You only look like him. You are a djinni!"

"Yes," the figure answers, growing larger still until it is ten feet tall. "I am a dead one, bound in my unlife to serve Master Rashad." As it enlarges, the image of Ubar wavers and falls from it like water cascading off a rock. In Ubar's place is a scantily-clad undead creature with inches-long fingernails, bony arms, and skeletal legs that end in horse's hooves. Its hair is a tangle of grays and browns that fall to its bony shoulders. The creature has the ears of a donkey, a wicked grin, and piercing black eyes.

"Die, Jamil, that my master will be happy and that I might return to my grave."

You spin on your heels and run smack into an invisible wall. The creature commands magic!

"Don't fight me, Jamil. I will make your death quick and painless." You hear the crunch of earth behind you as the undead djinni moves closer.

Whirling, you draw your cutlass, the one your guide created for you. "I'll not give in without a fight," you curse. "I've come too far!"

The creature ambles closer, its filthy clawlike hands reaching out as if to bat at you. You stand with your blade ready, but the undead djinni does not come close enough for you to strike out. Instead, its fingernails glow red, and its black eyes burn like fire. A great gout of flame leaps from its hands, and you fall to the ground as the fire licks above your head.

"Stand still, Jamil," the dead thing scolds.

You roll toward the thing, bringing your blade out and slicing at the creature's skeletal legs. The blade finds its mark, but bounces harmlessly off the creature's bones.

"Foolish mortal," the undead djinni cackles. "Even living, you are not my match."

Your mind dances. If the sha'ir sent this creature here, then the sha'ir won the battle with the yak-man on the mountain. You spring to your feet and jump back as the undead djinni's claws rake the air.

You bring the blade up again, this time slicing at the creature's arm with all your might. Again the weapon finds its mark, but this time it cuts through the bone. The clawlike hand falls to the alley floor, and the creature howls.

"That will cost you a painful death, Jamil," the dead djinni rants. With that, the creature disappears, leaving you alone in the alley.

"Whew!" you gasp, pleased with yourself that you scared it away. You turn to exit the alley, and unfortunately find yourself face-to-face with the undead djinni again.

"Can't I get rid of you?"

"Only by dying," the thing hisses. This time when the creature lashes out with its remaining claw, it successfully strikes, cutting through the fabric on your sleeve and scratching your arm.

"Ow!" The cut burns like fire, and you grit your teeth to ignore the pain.

The dead djinni presses its attack, bending over to get closer to you and bringing its arm up for another swing. With the speed and agility of a cat, you dart in, jump up, and bring the blade down across the creature's neck. The metal slices through the bone, and the dead djinni's head falls to the alley stones. Its bony body stands convulsing and quivering, then it topples forward to join its head, and you barely have time to get out of its way.

"Yuck," you state, looking at the rotting, headless

corpse. Peering out of the alley, you see passersby lost
in their conversations. Apparently your struggle went
unnoticed.

You clean your blade on the creature's meager garments and step out into the street. The warmth of the
sun feels good against your face, and you notice the
pain from the cut on your arm is fading.

There is the youth, his attention caught by a man
making a monkey perform for a small crowd. You
quickly join the boy.

"Where have you been?" the boy asks, pointing at
the torn fabric of your sleeve.

"Ran into someone I thought was an old friend,"
you reply, then usher the boy away from the monkey.
"We had a disagreement."

The questions die on the youth's tongue as he again
gets caught up in the sights and sounds of the marketplace. He points to various buildings and describes the
wares found inside.

An idea crosses your mind. You remember the boy
mentioning the singing barber. If the barber is going to
sing for the Grand Caliph today, perhaps you could
find a way to go with him—that would get you inside
the palace. You've come so far that you can't quit now.

Again, the feeling of being watched persists, and
you nudge the boy into the shadows toward the barbershop, hoping to catch a glimpse of who is watching
you. Perhaps it is someone from the al-Dinak warehouse, fearful that you are kidnapping the youth. Perhaps it is someone from the yellow warehouse, piqued
with interest over your search for a simple blue bottle.
Perhaps it is another creature sent by the sha'ir.

Then you see him—the watcher—a cloaked figure
across the street. The form is vaguely familiar and
draped in dark clothes, but a trio of chattering girls walks
in front of him, and when they pass by, he is gone.

"Thanks for your help," you say to the boy as you
approach the barbershop. "But it's time we part company. I've found a way inside the palace."

The boy grins and loses himself in the crowd, and

you head toward the barber, who is closing his shop and locking the front door.

"Excuse me, barber," you say hurriedly as you approach, casting a glance over your shoulder to make sure you are not being watched. "I am Jamil from Jumlat, City of Multitudes. A visitor in town, I have heard wonderful things about your skill with a razor."

"Sorry, young man," the barber intones in a deep, melodic voice. "I am practicing another skill in but an hour. If you come back tomorrow I will be happy to serve you." He starts to walk away, but again you interrupt him.

"Sir, it is this other skill that I am interested in. I know you sing. Your voice is legendary. And I have come all the way from the City of Multitudes to hear you perform. I spent my last dinar getting here, and these are the only clothes I have left. I, too, am a singer, and it would mean so much to me if I could hear you."

The barber smiles broadly, showing a front tooth of gold that sparkles in the sunlight. You notice his graying black hair is expertly trimmed, and his beard is even and waxed to a point. He reaches a hand to stroke his beard, and you note his fingers are encrusted with jeweled rings. Indeed, his clothes also proclaim his wealth. The barber's caftan is a thick brocade material, expensive though not flamboyant. Elegant, you decide as you see tiny black pearls that are sewn along the edge of his collar.

"You have come all this way just to hear me sing?"

You nod enthusiastically, surprised that your story has convinced him so far. "Why, yes! Musicians in Jumlat speak so highly of you that I had to hear you for myself. I risked all my possessions in an attempt to meet you and see you perform. Please do not disappoint me. Let me hear you sing today."

His grin grows even broader. "Why, yes, young man . . . "

"Jamil."

"Yes, Jamil, I will sing for you. But not here. The marketplace has not the acoustics, and I do not want to tax my voice before my performance today. Why don't you come with me? I am performing at the palace for the Grand Caliph. I will need someone to come with me and carry my barber tools, for I have also promised to tend to the Grand Caliph's hair." He points to a satchel at his feet and indicates you should pick it up.

"Yes!" you exclaim, quickly grabbing it. Despite the size of the satchel, it is relatively light. "To go to the palace with you would be such an honor."

"I am a friend of the Grand Caliph," the barber politely brags. "He enjoys my singing, and I enjoy his fine hospitality. Why, nowhere else have I tasted dates so sweet as in the courtyard of the Grand Caliph's palace."

You listen enthusiastically to the barber as you make your way through the rest of the Grand Bazaar. You decide you could enjoy living here. And, indeed, you might spend many, many days here if you can't find the blue bottle quickly—and the marid inside. After all, you haven't the coin to get back to Jumlat. And even if you found your way home to the City of Multitudes, it is unlikely Essaf the Hungry would hire you again; you would have to seek your fortune with another pearl captain. It is unfortunate the City of Delights does not seem to have a pearling trade.

The barber drones on in one of the most pleasant voices you have ever heard. "I would say, Jamil, and there would be few in the City of Delights who would argue with me, that the palace of the Grand Caliph is the most exquisite and impressive building in Golden Huzuz. Oh, and Jamil, make sure you address the building and its owner correctly."

You look at him quizzically.

An explanation is not long in coming.

"The Palace of the Grand Caliph. You can call it that. But it is also named the Seat of the Enlightened Throne and the Lair of the Great Enlightened, for the Grand Caliph is one of the most enlightened individuals in all of Golden Huzuz, and he is a lion among men. He has many titles, all of them most appropriate. The Grand Caliph is Khalil al-Assad al-Zahir, a man most assuredly chosen by Fate and the gods to be here in Golden Huzuz. He is the Worthy of the Gods, Scourge of the Unbelievers, Defender of the Faithful, Confidant of Djinn, and Master of the Enlightened Throne."

"Djinn?"

"Yes. He has many djinn within the palace."

"And he commands them all?"

"Not exactly," the barber laughs, clearly amused at your ignorance. "Most are free to come and go as they please, although some serve him by design or contract. The Grand Caliph does not believe in slavery and will have no slave—man or djinni—within his palace walls."

"But he has djinn . . ." you mumble to yourself, wondering if the djinni who is king of the Citadel of Ten Thousand Pearls roams within the palace walls of his own volition, is secretly a slave to the caliph, or is still in the blue bottle.

"Djinn interest you?"

"No. Not really. I think they only cause trouble for people."

The barber laughs again, a deep, sonorous sound that reverberates in the street. The tone causes passersby to look—including a passerby that is somehow familiar to you.

Yes! The dark-clad watcher. You spin to look at him more closely, but he is gone again.

"Barber . . ."

"Yes, Jamil, we are being watched. I know not the man, but I suspect he is a common thief wanting to steal my jewelry. Do not fear, young man. My skill with a scimitar matches my skill at song and shaving." He pats the weapon at his side, and you note that the blade's hilt is gold and has sapphires and emeralds embedded in the hilt.

"But enough talk of thieves and djinn," the barber guffaws. "Behold the gates of the Palace of the Enlightened Throne!"

You and the barber pass through the gates and enter what the barber calls the "first court, or the Court of Enlightenment." A city within a city. There are no other words to describe it.

Guards are all about, carrying scimitars as long as you are tall. The sharp blades glint in the sunlight and make you nervous. Glancing upward along the thick walls that surround the palace, you spot a pair of djinn. Standing roughly twelve feet tall, they appear to watch all those in the entry court.

The barber notices your discomfort and chuckles. "Jamil, the guards and the djinn won't hurt you unless you try to harm the Grand Caliph or steal from the palace. Only the foolish would try to steal from the Master of the Enlightened Throne, though there have been thefts here during my lifetime. In fact, almost a year ago to this very day a scribe who worked here ran away with ten thousand gold dinars."

"He wasn't caught?" You find a glimmer of hope.

"No, not yet. But there is a reward. The Grand Caliph has promised half of what was stolen—five thousand dinars—to the man or woman who can capture the thief. The Grand Caliph no longer cares about the missing gold coins; he just wants to make sure the thief is punished. It will discourage others from stealing."

You swallow hard and look ahead, taking in the sights and sounds of an open court filled with manicured grass and sculpted trees. Orchids hang from branches, scenting the air.

"Beautiful," you whisper, envying those who live within the palace grounds.

"Yes, and it is always so," the barber muses. "Magic covers the palace grounds, letting rain in only when the Grand Caliph desires. It is always warm and wonderful inside. Ah, perhaps some day I will take Khalil up on his offer to live here. But for now I fear I would miss all the activity of the Grand Bazaar."

"Gorar!" shouts a young man roughly your age. Dressed in a caftan even more elaborate than the barber's,

he rushes up and bows before your companion. "The Grand Caliph is waiting with his four wives. Your songs will make the day glorious for them."

"Well then," laughs the barber. "Let us be off to the Grand Caliph. Come along, Jamil, we cannot keep the Scourge of the Unbelievers waiting."

You hurry after the barber and soon find yourself deeper in the courtyard, where more guards with shining swords are posted and djinn patrol the walls and paths. Seated on a dais with four beautiful women curled up at his side is the Grand Caliph. His eyes dance when he spots the barber, and he stands to greet his friend. The barber bows in respect, then clasps hands with Khalil, the most powerful man in all of Golden Huzuz.

"Who is this, friend barber?" the Grand Caliph waves a hand toward you, and you realize all attention is focused on you for the moment.

"A new friend!" Gorar exclaims. "He is one who has come from afar to learn to sing from a master."

"Then let us hope the gods bless him with as rich a voice as you, my friend." The caliph returns to his seat, and the barber motions for you to back away. He begins to sing a slow, rich song, drawing the attention of all those in the courtyard. Indeed, even the guards and the djinn watch him.

You have an opportunity here. You could sneak away and lose yourself in the courtyard. There are so many people in the palace that they would not notice one young man skirting about. This could be your chance to find the blue bottle. Granted, it might take you a while, as there must be many chambers and courtyards to search. Still, this is what you came to Huzuz for—to free the king of the Citadel of Ten Thousand Pearls.

You have another option, Jamil, one that might prove easier. You could tell the Grand Caliph of your plight. If he is the man the barber claims, one opposed to slavery, he might help you. If the marid is free within the palace walls, he might encourage the genie to go home to Tala, his wife. If the marid is still trapped in the blue bottle, he might give you the flask so you can complete your great task. Or he might open the blue bottle and capture the wishes for himself. And what if he no longer has the bottle?

So much to think about and consider, young pearl diver. What will you do?

If you slip away into the palace grounds to start your search, turn to 46.

If you decide to tell the Grand Caliph about the king of the Citadel of Ten Thousand Pearls, turn to 62.

49

The fourth wife of the Grand Caliph told you to go straight, and be careful not to get lost. The door straightest in your path when you entered the hall was the one made of oak, and you head for it now.

You reach forward and grasp the polished brass knob. Turning it, you step inside and see display case upon display case filled with the glass shapes of griffins, hippogriffs, pegasi, and other statues. They shimmer in the magical light of a glowing glass orb in the center of the ceiling. The fourth wife of the Grand Caliph was taking you to see her favorites—the glass griffins. A tall, broadshouldered guard stands like a statue in the far corner of the room. Beyond the guard is another door, similar to the one you just entered. Perhaps you should go on, continue your straight path, or perhaps you should go back and try another door in the hallway.

"What do you want?" the guard asks none too politely.

"I am the Grand Caliph's glassblower," you announce, maintaining your ruse. "The fourth wife of the Grand Caliph directed me this way to view his works of glass."

"Yes, the fourth wife favors this room," the guard

says. "She comes here nearly every day to look at the griffins. Only the beautiful glass griffins."

You fold your hands together nervously and glance about the room. "Actually, I am here to look at his vases and bottles. I want to start with a few simple creations, and I want to complement what the Enlightened One already has."

The guard nods toward the far oak door.

Do you continue on to that door, hoping what you seek is beyond? If so, turn to 64.

Do you fear the guard is trying to trap you, and so excuse yourself to try another door? If you go to the cherrywood door, turn to 43. If you select the walnut door, turn to 57.

50

You must get that carpet back! You might need it to find the bottle where the king of the Citadel of Ten Thousand Pearls is captive.

Besides, you will not allow someone to steal from you, even if that someone *is* a djinni! You leave the docks in a huff and strike out across the warehouse district of Golden Huzuz. You vow to find that djinni and get your carpet back. Then you'll go after the bottle, free the king inside, and make him teach that mischievous djinni a lesson!

The hours melt away, and you walk up and down the streets. Often your glance turns skyward and you hope to spot another flying carpet with the thieving djinni as a guide.

By nightfall, you still have not found him, nor do you have a place to sleep. You curl up in the doorway of a closed shop. You see other poor people doing the same thing. You'll be safe. You have no dinars for someone to hassle you over, and you no longer have a valuable, magical carpet. Drifting off into a troubled sleep filled with laughing djinn, demanding djinn, and a sad-looking green sea djinni, you get little rest.

Before dawn, you are roused by a pair of large, rough hands that pin you to the doorway.

"Good one, huh? Young. Strong. I feel muscles in his arms. Got the look of the sea about him."

"Cap'n'll be pleased," another replies.

"Let me go!" you scream.

But the man who grabbed you laughs. He is huge, nearly seven feet tall, and ugly as an old sea bass. His arms are covered with muscles and tattoos, and you cannot break his impossibly strong grip.

"Aha, lad! Don't fight me. Cap'n will be happy to see you. Put you to work. But no pay. Not for you." He chuckles sinisterly.

"No! Stop!" you shout as you continue to struggle in an effort to break his grip. The beggars and youths sleeping in the other doorways glance up, then pretend to go back to sleep. Kidnapping people in the middle of the night obviously is nothing new in Huzuz.

"Where are you taking me?" you stammer, still attempting to wrench free.

His fingers dig into your arm a little tighter. "To Cap'n Waleed—slave," he barks. "The cap'n needs more deckhands. He'll let you go after a year or two. Or three." The man tilts his head back and laughs loud and long. His partner trails behind, also bringing a reluctant "recruit."

You curse yourself for foolishly trying to find a lone djinni in a city so large. You should have stuck to your goal of finding the bottle. You could have done it without the carpet. You suspected it was somewhere in the yellow warehouse—or at the very least in one of the warehouses nearby. Now you will have no opportunity to find the king, and you might never see Jumlat or Huzuz, City of Delights, again. City of Delights, hah! City of Slavery. City of Thieving Djinni. You pray the man is right. You hope Captain Waleed will set you free in a year.

THE END

51

No, you'll not back down now. You'll steal into the big yellow warehouse and find the king's bottle. No one will bother to report the theft of a simple blue glass flask.

Like a monkey, you scamper up the crates piled outside the window and pry the pane open. It takes a little work to jimmy it loose, as the building is made well and is in excellent repair. It is evident the al-Farif family has a considerable amount of dinars to their name. Climbing inside, you enter a place as dark as the cave beneath the desert.

Gingerly lowering yourself to the floor, you grope about with your hands and find shelves.

There are shelves everywhere. The scent of spices fills your nose and makes your eyes water. The scent is overpowering, and it makes you sneeze.

How are you going to find a bottle in all of this?

Reaching your arms higher, you pad tentatively forward, using your fingertips to guide you. Your fingertips brush over sanded wood shelves, boxes, glass bottles, canvas sacks. There must be lanterns hung about so the workers can see to stock the shelves when the sky is overcast.

You travel only a few more feet when your right hand brushes over a smooth glass lantern with a polished metal bottom. You fumble with it and freeze like a statue when you think you hear a footstep nearby.

You listen for several moments. Nothing. Perhaps a mouse. Perhaps something on the shelf settling.

Satisfied you are alone, you coax the wick to light. The lantern casts an eerie glow about the place and reveals more shelves filled with spices.

You hold the lantern close to your body and make your way up and down the aisles of the warehouse. Most of the spices are in jars and flasks and bear carefully printed labels. Peering closer, you note the name of the merchant the spice belongs to and when it was stored. Every bottle and container is marked.

And that means Sha'ir Rashad al-Azzazi's blue bottle should be marked as well. No use checking every shelf. There must be records somewhere. Making your way to the front of the warehouse, you find an office. It is a cluttered room dominated by a large desk virtually covered with sheets of vellum. You carefully place the lantern on the desk and begin to sort through the paper.

"It must be here somewhere," you whisper.

"Indeed, whatever you are looking for probably is," a deep voice replies.

Whirling, you see a massive, muscular man—and two other men behind him. Clad in common robes, each carries a large scimitar—all of which are drawn.

"Thievery is not looked kindly upon in Golden Huzuz, stranger. We hope you find the City of Delights's jail as accommodating as our employer's warehouse."

You bolt from the desk and fly to the front door, only to find it locked and a pair of hands on your shoulders. You struggle, but they are too strong for you. The men easily pick you up and carry you off into the night.

"Stupid little thief," the muscular man scolds. "You will serve many years in the Huzuz jail all because you were foolish enough to break into a warehouse."

How could I not have considered the possibility of guards? you berate yourself. Your head was too full of visions of djinn and treasure. Well, you will have plenty of time to clear your head in jail.

THE END

52

"Very well," you steam, realizing it is pointless to argue with a djinni. "You can have the flying carpet—though you certainly don't need it. You can fly without one."

Despite your reluctance, you know that with a flick of his wrist he could send you to who-knows-where. You roll up the rug and toss it at him. He catches it with no effort and grins broadly.

"You are wise, young man. You will do well in life. Wise men realize that riches do not always make one wealthy."

Your puzzled expression causes him to laugh.

"You will see what I mean, Jamil. Now, I must be off. I sense another carpet in the air—hopefully one driven by someone with plenty of dinars to spare." With that, the djinni whirls about like a top and springs into the air.

You watch his form retreat into the brilliant Huzuz sky, and you shudder. Far above is a black carpet that sends shivers racing up and down your spine. But why? I am foolish to worry over another visitor to Huzuz, you scold yourself.

You turn your attention to the yellow warehouse. It will be a little more difficult to find the bottle without the rug pointing the way, but you remember what the other djinni's bottle looked like. Tala said this bottle would look the same. You pad to the warehouse door.

Turn to 16.

53

Spotting a group of merchants, you quickly slip into their ranks and pass inside the gate unchallenged. You are relieved to make it inside the palace grounds without being stopped; you did not have a tale fabricated explaining your presence. Glancing upward, you spot a dozen or more guards on the walls, each with a scimitar as long as you are tall. The keen blades glint in the sunlight. Beyond them are a pair of genies, probably djinn of the desert judging by their bald heads and ruddy complexions. They, too, wield scimitars, with blades at least six feet long. They are taller than twelve feet, and their muscles sheen with sweat in the hot sun. You will be careful not to run afoul of them, for you doubt you would breathe much longer.

Passing through a chamber with polished black marble walls, you and the merchants step out into a courtyard filled with perfectly sculpted trees and manicured grass. Beautiful blooms of orchids—pink, purple, and white—hang from the branches and scent the air.

The merchants take a path to the southeast, and you follow them, finding yourself cooled by a breeze that exists in the courtyard but was not present in the city outside. You suspect powerful magic is at work here. Throughout the courtyard you see more guards, all armed with long, sharp scimitars. Their eyes dart about everywhere, making sure they account for all visitors inside the palace walls.

As you glance about the courtyard, taking everything in, you spy the familiar dark-clad form of the man who was watching you in the Grand Bazaar. This time there are no shadows or shoppers to block your view of him. His dark eyes meet your stare. He is familiar, but you cannot place him. He steps forward, and a hand reaches inside his robe. His eyes do not leave yours.

A chill races up and down your spine. The sha'ir! He is the young Sha'ir Rashad al-Azzazi. How could he have gotten here? Foolish question, you chide yourself. He commands magic. He can go anywhere he wants.

Before you can react, you spot a guard striding toward him.

"What is your business here?" the guard barks at the sha'ir.

The sha'ir mumbles something. He is too far away for you to hear what he is saying. Whatever he said, there was magic in it. Before the guard can reach his side, the sha'ir disappears in a puff of gray smoke. Other guards rush forward, searching through the bushes and the trees.

You continue your path, your eyes darting everywhere, looking for the sha'ir. Ahead you see other merchants, showing wares to buyers dressed in elaborate clothes. No doubt the buyers are acting on the Grand Caliph's behalf.

   While you watch the transactions, you mull over
what to do next. You must find the blue bottle and
avoid the sha'ir. You've come too far to turn back. You
could wander away from the merchants and explore
the rooms and courtyards of this grand place. It will
take a while, you realize, and perhaps you will never
find the bottle. But not to look would be to ignore
everything you have accomplished so far.
   As you think about the possibilities and worry
about the sha'ir, a voice cuts through the air. It is rich
and melodious, and it sings of fair Zakhara and the
sands that whip across the desert. You notice that the
guards have turned their attention toward the center of
the courtyard, where the voice is coming from.
   Now is your chance. You will slip away from the
merchants and explore the palace.

   Turn to 46.

54

Pursuing the mischievous djinni would be foolish. After all, refusing to give him the carpet ended you up in the harbor—soaking wet and minus the carpet anyway. Besides, it should not be too difficult to find the flask. You suspect it is in the large yellow warehouse, as that is the building the carpet was descending over, and you remember what Tala's bottle looked like. Hopefully this one will look the same.

It is not a far walk to the warehouse district. In a way, you are thankful for the djinni's tour. Otherwise you would not know the flask was in a warehouse or even where the warehouse district was. Perhaps Fate put you in the hands of the djinni. It is just too bad you didn't cooperate with him a little more.

By the time you reach the warehouse district, your clothes and hair are dry. The sea water did not harm your embroidered caftan. Looking a little more closely at the garment, you note that it is worth several dinars, more than you could have afforded to spend in the Jumlat marketplace. The cutlass, too, is more sword than you could have afforded.

You smile and pad to the warehouse door.

Turn to 16.

55

Following the beautiful girl's directions, you find the al-Dinak warehouse. It looks nothing like the big yellow warehouse you just left. This building is in disrepair, a shambles. Paint is peeling everywhere, and the roof sags. You stop a passerby outside the open front door to make sure you have the right place.

"Yes," a man says solemnly. You can tell by his hands and weathered face that he is likely a longtime dock worker. "This is the warehouse of the al-Dinak

family. It is the only one they have left. The family fell
on hard times when they became sworn enemies of the
al-Danifi family, which also runs a warehousing operation. The al-Dinak family sold off another of its warehouses last week. It is over there." He points at a
building in even worse condition. "I know not who
bought that one, but I have heard the one behind us,
their last warehouse, is for sale as well. I am sure the
family would part with it cheaply."

Doubtful the al-Dinaks still have the bottle, you
think. As you shuffle through the front door, your eyes
meet those belonging to a dirty youth.

"Store something for you, sir? We have the best
rates in all of Golden Huzuz. Our handlers will not
drop any of your goods, and we will guard them well,
as if our lives depended on their safety." The youth
puffs out his chest and grins. You guess he is eight or
nine years old.

You can't help but smile back. "Actually, I'm looking
for something stored here—or that was stored here."

The youth scowls and scratches at an insect bite on
his arm. "Well, you're welcome to check our records. I
don't read that well. Or, you can wait for my father.
He's at the docks trying to drum up business."

You pat his head. "Let's not bother your father. I'm
certain he's a very busy man."

The youth beams. "I'll help you. The other man did-
n't want me to help. He's coming back later when my
father is here."

"Other man?" The hairs on the back of your neck
stand up.

"Yeah. A man dressed in black. Said he was looking
for a bottle."

You shiver, but the youth doesn't notice your reac-
tion. He points to a jumble of crates, all filled with
scroll tubes and pieces of parchment, obviously the
warehouse records. This is going to take a while, you
decide. You sit in front of the mass of parchment and
begin looking through the records. Although it might
be easier to simply search the warehouse, you're not

certain the workers would allow that, and you're not certain you'd have any better luck. Besides, after seeing inside the al-Farif warehouse, you'd rather start with records than shelves.

The youth sits next to you and regales you with tales of how great a businessman his father is. You nod and smile and continue to scan the records until your eyes light on a sheet of parchment. Your spirits sink low.

"No," you moan, staring at the parchment. You fold it and stick it inside your pocket. It would do no good for the man in black to find this.

"What's wrong?" the boy chatters, stopping his story.

You slump against the crates and sadly laugh. "For decades a blue bottle sat in one of your competitor's warehouses. And for only one month did it sit in yours—with a collection of glassware."

"So? You're looking for a blue bottle, too? I'll help you find it. I know every inch of the warehouse." The youth grins. "That's what the man in black is looking for. Blue bottles must be popular today. I'll bet we can find a blue bottle somewhere in this warehouse."

You grimace, perturbed about the information in the records—and the "man in black."

"You don't understand," you begin. "According to these records, it's not here. Two days ago a buyer for the Grand Caliph purchased all of your glassware, including my blue bottle."

"We have other bottles. And there's even more in the marketplace! I'll help you find a pretty blue one."

You smile at the boy. "No. I needed a particular bottle. Not just any one will do. And now the Grand Caliph has what I am looking for, and I shall never have it. I shall always be poor."

"Never is a bad word, and poor is only a temporary state," the youth announces, poking out his lip and staring at the mess of parchments you made during your search. "Kamu al-Danifi said he would ruin my father. Said we would never do business in this town.

He almost ruined us. Almost. But we'll make it. My father is getting more contracts every day. Why, yesterday he took this warehouse off the selling block. My father doesn't quit."

"Well, I'll not quit, either, my young friend. I guess I'll go to the Grand Caliph and see about getting my blue bottle."

"May I come, too?" the youth asks excitedly. "I know the way to the palace. I know the City of Delights very, very well."

That's up to you, Jamil. Do you want a boy tagging along with you? He'd be liable to get in the way. On the other hand, he says he knows Golden Huzuz, City of Delights. You certainly don't know the city. He could serve as a guide, and—unlike the djinni—he probably wouldn't ask for anything.

If you take the boy with you, turn to 48.

If you think you can find the palace from your sky-ward tour and would prefer going alone, turn to 41.

56

Better go back for the boy, you think. He knows the city. And he probably knows better than you how to get inside the palace grounds.

You retrace your steps.

"It's you again!" the youth exclaims. "So you need my help after all, huh? I guessed you would, being a stranger to Golden Huzuz. Besides, I've been to the palace. In fact, I've been just about everywhere in the city."

He shuffles some parchment and puts it in a crate. Brushing off his robe, he grins broadly at you. "I'll be glad to help you find your way to the palace, and inside, too, if you desire. Well?"

You nod yes, thankful to have a little assistance in the City of Delights. Besides, you learned your way around Jumlat, City of Multitudes, before you were his age.

The boy scampers out the door, and motions for you to follow.

Turn to 48.

57

Stepping through the walnut door decorated with the carvings of djinn, you enter a small courtyard dominated by a fountain. The water is multicolored, and you find yourself staring at it. Ringing the fountain are four crystal statues, the envious creation of a true glassblower. One is a statue of a desert djinni, and from his mouth pours a stream of rose-colored water.

Another is a statue of a sea djinni, this one a female, though looking not at all like the beautiful Tala you accidentally rescued. From her mouth pours water of the palest blue. From the mouth of a statue of a fire djinni comes orange water that bubbles and hisses with heat. And from the mouth of the final statue, a djinni that bears a close resemblance to the one who gave you a flying tour of the city, comes a stream of emerald green water. The colored water mixes in the center of the fountain, twirls and whirls, and takes your breath away with its uncommon appearance.

No such creation exists in Jumlat! If nothing else, you tell yourself, this trip to the City of Delights has shown you wonders to regale your friends with for weeks upon weeks.

Surrounding the fountain are tiny pink and lavender blooms, polished cobblestone patios, and blades of grass cut close to the ground. Not a single weed has found its way into this courtyard, you muse as you tear your eyes away from the fountain to an ebonwood door beyond.

"Perhaps the bottles are stored there," you mutter. "Or perhaps they are beyond one of the doors that I did not choose in the hallway behind me."

"Or perhaps I already have the bottle."

You whirl to face the speaker—the Sha'ir Rashad al-Azzazi.

"You are undone, Jamil. You will pay for interfering in my life. Prepare to die."

You gasp as the sha'ir wiggles his fingers, and a blue bolt shoots forth from his hands. You brace yourself for the impact of the magical force, knowing you cannot get out of the way in time, but you are astonished as the bolt swerves around you. Casting a glance over your shoulder, you see the bolt strike the fountain behind you. A blue glow covers the glass statues of the djinn. The glass statues sparkle, move, and detach themselves from the fountain.

The animated glass djinn are moving toward you!

You stare incredulously, your surprise costing you precious moments. The statues clink forward on glass feet, their glass hands outstretched and clawing at the air in front of them. You turn, drawing your sword and planting your feet wide apart. Then you risk a glance behind you to see what the sha'ir is doing.

Gone.

He's nowhere to be seen.

The glass soldiers move closer. *Clink . . . clink . . . clink . . .* over the cobblestones in the small courtyard. You see the sunlight glint off their long fingernails— they could impale you on those things!

As the first statue reaches you, you bring your blade down squarely on its shoulder, cleaving off an arm that falls to the cobblestones and shatters. The statue's other arm gets past your weapon, and the glass fingernails rake your chest.

"Argh!" The pain is intense, and you nearly double over in agony. You bite your lip to concentrate.

Again the statue lashes out with its remaining arm, and once again you swing your blade. This time the sword strikes the statue at its waist, cutting the thing in two and sending slivers of glass everywhere.

You close your eyes and throw your free arm across your face to prevent the glass shards from hurting you, but in the next moment, you realize your actions were a mistake. Two more of the statues reach you. They are cunning for things of glass. They position themselves to either side of you so you can only strike one at a time.

You'll oblige them, you decide. You bring your blade down upon the one to your right, confident that one swing will shatter this construct. No! The glass djinni jumped to the side, faster than you imagined it could move! Your blade cleaves the air, and you cry in pain when a glass hand thrusts at your left side, the nails digging into your flesh just above the waist. The other glass djinni!

You pivot, wielding the blade like a scythe as you turn, and the sword finds its mark. The head of the glass djinni to your left is cut free from the statue's body and sails across the courtyard to land in a bed of pink flowers. The headless body continues its assault, however, its glass hands that sparkle in the sunlight closing about your left arm.

"No!" you bark, bringing your sword down on the headless statue, cutting it neatly in two from neck to waist. The glass creation shatters, just as you feel glass nails jab at your back. The remaining two statues!

Spinning, you find two glass djinn raking their nails through your embroidered caftan. If the material were not so thick, it would have been your skin that was shredded. You raise your foot and push out against one of the statues, while you bring the blade up to cut off the leg of the other. Unable to stand, the one-legged statue falls to the cobblestones and breaks into hundreds of pieces.

But the statue you kicked did not budge. And now you find yourself in a predicament. The sole surviving glass djinni has grabbed your foot. Tugging hard, it spills you to the courtyard floor. Your sword flies from your hand, and the glass statue presses its attack.

You struggle to rise, but the statue places a heavy glass foot upon your chest. It presses hard, and you realize with horror it means to kill you by caving in your ribs!

In a desperate attempt to live, you grab the statue's leg, cutting yourself on the sharp edges. Ignoring the pain, you pull and unbalance the thing. Bringing up your legs, you kick out at it, and at last your efforts are rewarded as it tumbles off you and shatters when it strikes the cobblestones.

Jumping to your feet, you rush to your sword, scoop it up, then glance about the courtyard for the sha'ir and more glass statues.

Nothing. Just shards of glass. Were the statues simply a diversion so he could go after the bottle?

You stare at the statueless fountain for several long moments. Then you hear voices coming from somewhere behind you. No doubt others are approaching this section of the palace, curious about the sounds of breaking glass. You must make a decision quickly, Jamil.

Do you go forward to the ebonwood door beyond the fountain? If so, turn to 60.

Do you return to the hall and slip inside the cherry-wood door, which is closest? If so, flip to 43.

Do you rush back to the oak door to hide behind it? If so, turn to 49.

58

Nodding to the guard and the Grand Caliph, you open this door and step inside.

Yes! Your heart leaps.

There are vases and bottles on shelves upon shelves upon shelves. Shelves that reach the ceiling nearly fifteen feet above the polished marble floor.

You can see all the glassware perfectly, as a globe of magical light suspended from the mahogany ceiling above illuminates everything evenly.

Clear glass. Rose-colored glass. Glass the color of midnight. There are so many hues of glass, and in so many, many shapes. You try to take it all in.

"Hundreds," you whisper, selecting the bottom shelf to your right and inspecting as many of the containers as you can at once. Some are sealed, some have loose-fitting tops. Some have no tops at all. A few have liquid inside, probably perfumes or fine liqueurs.

Your eyes blur from the numbers and colors and sizes and . . .

"There!" you exclaim.

"Success, Jamil?" you hear the caliph ask. He and the guard pad into the room.

"Yes," you say excitedly, reaching for a blue bottle on the bottom shelf. With the other, thicker bottles in front of it, the fluted glass was nearly hidden. It looks for all of Zakhara like the twin of the bottle you found on the bottom of the Golden Gulf. You fall to your knees and gingerly extend your hand to clasp its neck. Carefully moving the other bottles out of the way, you feel the smoothness of the glass.

Sitting cross-legged on the floor, you pull the bottle toward you and hold it with both hands. The seal is tight, but you notice the caliph and the guard make no move to help you. After all, the caliph said this was *your* quest. You tug and tug and tug and fail to pull it free.

"Hmmm," you think aloud, "how to get this open?" You tug one last time, then set the bottle down in front of you and reach under your caftan for your pearling knife. It has stayed with you through all your adventures. The edge is still sharp, and you use it to pierce the bottle's seal, running the blade around the top until you feel it loosen in your hand. Replacing the knife, you tug on the top again and fall backward when a billow of sea foam escapes.

"Free!" shouts a spray of gray-green mist that erupts from the bottle. "I'm free!" The mist dances and whirls, twirls upward like a cyclone, and brightens to a dazzling, mesmerizing emerald green. "I . . . am . . . free!" The mist spins and changes color again, this time to a brilliant blue.

You are barely aware that the guard steps in front of the caliph and draws his weapon protectively.

The mist thickens and takes on a vaguely human shape. "Free!" the coalescing form of the sea djinni shouts in an ear-splitting tone that rattles the shelves. "After all these decades. FREE!" His booming voice shatters every piece of glass in the room and causes you to crouch to avoid the flying shards. Your action is useless, you are pelted by the pieces of glass, many chunks striking your arms and face and drawing blood.

The guard and the caliph throw their arms over their faces to keep the glass away from their eyes.

"Decades upon decades have I slept in that bottle, captured by my own foolishness!" The voice fills the room, and you cup your hands over your ears to deaden the noise. You notice the guard and the caliph are doing likewise.

The djinni is massive and commanding. With rippling blue muscles and arms as thick as posts, he stands in front of you, meaty fists on his hips. You glance upward into his angular face and see his bright blue eyes, the color of the Golden Gulf.

"Who has freed me?"

"J-J-Jamil," you answer, rising to your feet and carefully avoiding the glass all about you.

"My thanks, Jamil. You have ended an eternity of torture. Away from my wife. Away from my city. Away from all I held dear. My heart was as black as the bottom of the sea. Now to find my wife, Jamil. You must help me! She is captive in a bottle like mine. An evil sha'ir did this, a man who is expert at enslaving djinn. That is why I need your help. A human would be beneath his notice."

You try to interrupt him, but fail. The djinni rants on about how he and Tala were captured by the sha'ir in Sikak, City of Coins, and about how the sha'ir feared they would escape so he hid them away until he could grow more powerful. The sea djinni is oblivious to all but himself and has not even noticed you were cut by the flying glass. He does not even notice the caliph.

"The vicious sha'ir fashioned a map, Jamil," the djinni's voice booms. "Out of a carpet."

"I know," you state simply, finally getting his attention. "On the carpet he embroidered the locations of the flasks containing you and Tala. Your wife is safe. She's somewhere outside of Sikak, I suspect waiting for me.

She is waiting for you, too, hoping I would free you."

"And free me you did!" the djinni whoops. "And now I shall be reunited with my beloved. Again we will rule the Citadel of Ten Thousand Pearls!"

With that, the djinni's form dissolves into a spray of seafoam that thoroughly soaks you. The column of water shoots toward the ceiling and disappears.

"But what about my treasure?" you wail, looking at the broken glass all about you. "What about my dinars and pearls and my palace?"

"What about *my* palace?" the caliph says stonily. "I am a champion of freedom, Jamil. But these pieces were worth thousands of dinars." You grin sheepishly, not knowing what to say. The silence in the room is uncomfortable. After what seems an eternity, the caliph finally speaks. "Leave, Jamil," he states flatly. "Leave while I hold my anger in check."

You bow to him and cautiously pick your way from the room under his watchful eye. You pass by broken griffins and shattered hippogriffs.

Sundered beauty.

Outside you hear the pounding of footsteps. No doubt guards are on the way, drawn by the sound of breaking glass and the shouting djinni. You slip into the shadows, confident you can sneak away from the palace grounds. But something sharp poking your back dashes your plans.

"Where is my djinni, Jamil?" The voice is coarse and low, but you recognize it.

The voice belongs the Sha'ir Rashad al-Azzazi.

"I tire of following you, young thief. I want my carpet. And I want the king of the Citadel of Ten Thousand Pearls."

You're too late, you think as you feel the sharp object, a knife no doubt, prod your back again.

"You will take me to the bottle."

Turn to 63.

59

You'll not give the sha'ir the chance to kill you. You'll run! You throw your elbow backward, striking him in the chest. For a moment, he relaxes his grip on the knife at your back.

This is your chance. You sprint forward, your legs pumping hard to take you across the courtyard grass. Faster you run, passing guards who are jogging toward the caliph's glass rooms.

Dashing out the palace gates, you enter the streets of Huzuz. Your tired legs churn hard, sending you flying over the dirt and worked stone of the city streets.

He'll not have me, you think as you grasp your side, which hurts from running. You find comfort in the thought that he will also not have the king of the Citadel of Ten Thousand Pearls. You freed the king and the queen. You wrenched the djinn from the evil sha'ir's grasp.

You suppose that makes you a hero.

A fleeing hero.

"You are a dead man, Jamil."

The sha'ir! He's standing in the crowd in front of you! How did he get there? The evil wizard eyes you solemnly and weaves his fingers in the air before you can react.

"You are dead, Jamil, because soon I will be dead," he continues. His fingers dance through the air as he speaks. "The djinn you freed will return to kill me—revenge for my grandfather's imprisoning them. Revenge is important to djinn." His fingers wiggle faster.

You realize he is casting a spell, and you try to whirl on your heels. You have to put some distance between you and his magic. But you find yourself magically rooted to the spot, your feet stuck to the ground like bricks stuck together in a foundation, your toes numb.

"No!" you shout.

You notice his left hand has begun to glow red, the nails of his fingers growing longer and pointed, like sharp daggers.

Your mind screams, and you flail about futilely. You are no match for the evil wizard. You slam your eyes shut, not wanting to see your death coming. You pray fervently to Haku that your end will come quickly and with little pain.

One moment.

Two.

You feel a sharp jab of pain in your chest, and your eyes fly open to see the evil sha'ir thrusting his long, hot fingernails into your flesh.

"Enough!" you scream in pain, lashing upward with your fist. Your knuckles hit his lower arm strongly, and you knock his hand away.

The burning sensation subsides now that his magical fingernails are not boring into you.

"I've done nothing to you!" you blurt out angrily. "I have not hurt you. I have done nothing wrong."

"Wrong?" The sha'ir waves his arm about, indicating the street you stand rooted to. The crowd moves back, clinging to buildings and alley entrances. The people morbidly want to watch, not realizing they are in danger, too. "You've done nothing wrong? You invaded my palace, Jamil. You stole from me something of my grandfather's—a djinni worth a considerable fortune! Do you realize the wishes I could have squeezed from such a creature? Do you realize just what you stole from me?"

You swallow hard and pull at your feet. You are still stuck to the street. "You didn't even know about the djinni until I came along. I didn't *steal* anything. I merely set someone free."

"Fool!" the sha'ir bellows. He begins to waggle his fingers again. An evil grin plays across his face.

Sensation returns to your toes. You can move.

Move? You're flying!

The sha'ir's magic is causing you to rise in the air—above the city street. Higher and higher you go until you are above the rooftops and minarets. The people are small below.

But the sha'ir isn't small. The sha'ir is growing in size. Larger. Taller!

By the gods! The sha'ir must be twenty feet tall. And he's flying, too.

You hear the astonished gasps of the crowd below as the giant-sized Sha'ir Rashad al-Azzazi floats toward you, his outstretched hands easily strong enough to squeeze the breath from your lungs.

Thinking quickly, you fumble in the folds of your robe, and your fingers close upon your pearling knife. You keep your hand hidden, not wanting the evil man to know you are not helpless.

Effortlessly his form glides closer, like a cloud carried by a breeze. "This game is over, Jamil," he snarls as he closes in, his hand lashing out at you.

You duck below his fist and bring your own hand up, the blade of the pearling knife stabbing deep into his thick wrist. The sha'ir screams, more in surprise than agony, you suspect. No matter, you must press your momentary advantage.

Treating the air like water, you propel yourself forward in a favorite swimming stroke, as if you were diving for pearls in the Golden Gulf. You dart in toward his chest. Again your knife flashes upward.

This time the blade sinks into the flesh under his jaw. The sha'ir screams—now in pain. Blood spills from the wound and covers your hand. You tug the knife free and swing again.

Once more your blade finds its mark, this time in the giant-sized wizard's throat. But, he, too has struck. You feel the nails of his hands rake across your back. Like daggers, they dig into your skin, ripping your garment and flesh in one motion. The pain is intense, and you fear one more strike from him will end your life.

But the strike doesn't come.

His hands fly away from you, grabbing at his throat where your pearling knife rests.

"Jamil!" the sha'ir gasps, his eyes fluttering and his breath becoming ragged. "I cannot die," he croaks.

You see a trickle of blood appear at the corner of his massive mouth and realize your small weapon must

have dealt him a fatal blow, ripping through an artery in his throat.

His hands tremble and continue to grasp at the small wound you caused, from which blood is flowing freely. Then the hands stop moving. They fall to the giant sha'ir's side, and his mouth falls open as if he is sleeping.

He is dead.

And you are both falling to the streets below.

"No!" you scream. "I can't have won only to die!" The city street rushes up to meet the falling forms of you and the dead sha'ir. You close your eyes and pray the end will come quickly and without pain.

One moment.

Two.

You hear a loud, sickening thud. The body of Sha'ir Rashad al-Azzazi must have hit the city street. But you have not joined it.

You crack open an eye and see that you are hovering mere inches from the street, and only feet away from the broken corpse of the evil sha'ir.

Tala! She is in the crowd. It was she who, with her magic, stopped your fall. You see her grin at you and rush forward, and you feel yourself gently lowered to the street.

"My champion!" Tala gushes. "You saved my husband, and now we have saved you. Our debt is paid."

"The sha'ir will trouble no one any longer," the djinni king's deep voice cuts through the hubbub of Golden Huzuz.

"And now we must go," Tala interrupts. "It has been decades since we saw the Citadel of Ten Thousand Pearls. Farewell, Jamil."

The djinn wink at you, then they, too, grow. Ten feet. Twenty. The people gasp and back away.

Thirty.

"May Fate smile upon you!" the king calls.

The djinn's forms waver like mist, then turn to solid water.

The water churns and whirls like a cyclone, spraying salt water upon everyone on the street. The funnels

move up into the sky, disappearing in the clouds overhead. The citizens of the City of Delights stare at you
and the gigantic form of the dead sha'ir. You grin nervously at them and lose yourself in the crowd.

You've had a grand adventure, and you have your
skin. But you have no money and no way home. Huzuz
will be your home now. At least until you can raise
enough dinars to pay your way to Jumlat.

Perhaps they need pearl divers at the harbor.

THE END

60

You pull open the door made of ebonwood.

No! You have wandered into the barracks of the
guards! A dozen stop their conversations and games of
dice and rise as one. Two draw their scimitars and in a
few strides are in front of you. They were so engrossed
in their activities that they didn't hear your struggle
with the glass statues outside—or didn't care. And you
were too engrossed in your thoughts to bother to listen
at this door before you opened it.

"Trespasser!" one shouts. "How could one such as
you get into the inner chambers of the palace?"

Thinking quickly, you blurt out, "I'm not a trespasser. I've just been hired by the Grand Caliph, himself. I am a glassblower."

The guards eye you carefully, and then one barks.
"No. He lies. The Grand Caliph would not hire someone to blow glass. His wives enjoy shopping for glass-
works in the bazaar. Get the trespasser!"

You whirl on your heels and sprint across the courtyard, your feet crunching over the broken glass. But
the guards are just as quick. Several pairs of hands
grab you and hold you fast.

"Trespassing is a serious crime at this palace," the
tallest guard states flatly. "And those who commit the
crime must accept the penalty."

You swallow hard. "Penalty?"

"Death," he replies stonily. "Hold him!"

Two guards stand to each side of you, pinning your arms and legs in place. Despite your struggles, you cannot budge. They are as strong as elephants.

The tallest guard strides slowly forward and draws his blade.

"No!" you scream. He means to take off your head! Why did you have to open that door? Why didn't you pay attention to the woman's instructions and continue in a straight path?

He pulls back the blade, and it arcs quickly toward you, the metal glinting in the sun and stealing your life.

THE END

61

You'll not give the sha'ir the chance to kill you, but neither will you run from him. If you ran away now, you would be running from him the rest of your life. You'd be jumping at shadows, trusting no one. That would not be living.

You throw your elbow backward, striking him hard in the chest. Surprised, he relaxes his grip on the knife at your back and gives you an opening.

You whirl and slam your fist into his face.

"Fool!" he curses, as he spits out a tooth.

You have hurt him! You follow through and punch him again. This time you hit him solidly in the stomach, knocking the wind out of him and sending him flying to his rump.

The sha'ir raises his head, and his black eyes fix on yours. He wriggles the fingers on his right hand, and his palm begins to glow bright blue.

No! You can't let him cast a spell at you. Too late! A beam of blue light shoots forth from his palm, and you throw yourself to the grass. The beam sizzles in the air above your head, and you feel intense heat. If you had not moved, you might have been disintegrated!

Struggling to your feet, you notice the sha'ir is

already standing and is working more magic. He is weaving his fingers in the air in front of him and mumbling words you cannot understand. The caliph's guards give the pair of you a wide berth. They know magic is powerful, and they have no intention of running afoul of the sha'ir. It is obvious they will not help you. This is your fight.

"You are a dead man, Jamil." The evil wizard eyes you solemnly and gestures in the air. "You are dead, Jamil, because soon I will be dead," he continues, his fingers dancing before him as he speaks. "The djinni you freed will return to kill me—revenge for my grandfather's imprisoning him. Revenge is important to djinn. And to me." His fingers wiggle faster.

You try to whirl on your heels. You have to put some distance between you and his magic, enough distance to let you think. But you find yourself rooted to the spot, your feet magically stuck to the cobblestones of the palace courtyard like bricks stuck together in a foundation. Your toes are numb.

"No!" you shout.

You notice his left hand has begun to glow red, the nails of his fingers growing longer and pointed, like sharp daggers.

Your mind screams, and you flail about futilely. You are no match for the evil wizard. You slam your eyes shut, not wanting to see your death coming. You pray fervently to Haku that your end will come quickly and with little pain.

One moment.

Two.

You feel a sharp jab of pain in your chest, and your eyes fly open to see the evil sha'ir thrusting his long, hot fingernails into your flesh.

"Enough!" you scream in anguish, lashing upward with your fist. Your knuckles hit his lower arm strongly, and you knock his hand away.

The burning sensation subsides now that his magical fingernails are not boring into you.

"I've done nothing to you!" you blurt out angrily. "I

have not hurt you. I have done nothing wrong."

"Wrong?" The sha'ir waves his arm about, indicating the courtyard. The guards move back, sheltering behind the life-size statues. Too afraid to help you, they are also too morbidly curious to run. "You've done nothing wrong? You invaded my palace, Jamil. You stole from me something of my grandfather's—a djinni worth a considerable fortune. Do you realize the wishes I could have squeezed from such a creature? Do you realize just what you have stolen?"

You swallow hard and pull at your feet, but they are still stuck to the cobblestones. "You didn't even know about the djinni until I came along. I didn't *steal* anything! I merely set someone free."

"Fool!" the sha'ir bellows. He waggles his fingers again. An evil grin plays across his face.

Sensation returns to your toes. You can move.

Move? You're flying!

The sha'ir's magic is causing you to rise in the air—above the courtyard. Above the palace. Higher and higher you go until you are above the tallest rooftops and minarets of Golden Huzuz. The guards are small below.

But the sha'ir isn't small. The sha'ir is growing in size. Larger. Taller! By the gods! The sha'ir must be twenty feet tall. And *he's* flying, too!

You hear the astonished gasps of the guards below as Sha'ir Rashad al-Azzazi floats toward you, his outstretched hands strong enough to squeeze the breath from your lungs.

Thinking quickly, you fumble in the folds of your robe, and your fingers close upon your pearling knife. You keep your hand hidden, not wanting the evil man to know you are not completely helpless.

Effortlessly his form glides closer, like a cloud carried by a breeze. "This game is over, Jamil," he snarls as he closes, his hand lashing out.

You duck below his fist and bring your own hand up, the blade of the pearling knife stabbing deep into his wrist. The sha'ir screams, more in surprise than agony, you suspect. No matter, you must press your momentary advantage.

Treating the air like water, you propel yourself forward in a favorite swimming stroke, as if you were diving for pearls in the Golden Gulf. You dart in toward his chest. Again your knife flashes upward. This time the blade sinks into the flesh under his jaw.

The sha'ir screams—now in pain. Blood spills from the wound and covers your hand. You tug the knife free and swing again.

Indeed, you can sting!

Once more your blade finds its mark, this time in the giant-sized wizard's throat. But he, too, has struck. You feel the nails of his hands rake across your back. Like daggers, they dig into your skin, ripping your garment and flesh in one motion. You feel warmth on your back—the heat of your own blood. The pain is intense. One more strike and you will be dead!

But the strike does not come.

The sha'ir's hands fly away from you, grabbing at his throat where your pearling knife firmly rests.

"Jamil!" the sha'ir gasps, his eyes fluttering and his breath becoming ragged. "I cannot die," he croaks. "I . . . cannot . . ."

You see a trickle of blood appear at the corner of his massive mouth and realize your small weapon must have dealt him a fatal blow, ripping through an artery in his throat. His hands tremble and continue to grasp at the small wound you caused, from which blood is flowing freely. Then the hands stop moving. They fall to the giant sha'ir's side, and his mouth drops open as if he is sleeping.

He is dead.

And you are both falling to the courtyard below.

"No!" you scream. "I can't have won only to die!"

The cobblestones of the courtyard rush up to meet the falling forms of you and the dead sha'ir. You close your eyes and pray to Haku the end will come quickly and without pain.

One moment.

Two.

You hear a loud, sickening thud. The body of Sha'ir Rashad al-Azzazi must have hit first. But you have not joined it. In fact, you are no longer falling.

You crack open an eye and see that you are hovering inches above the cobblestones and feet away from the broken, giant corpse of the evil sha'ir.

Tala! She is next to a group of guards, and her husband stands nearby! It must have been they who stopped your fall with their magic.

The guards rush forward, no longer frightened of the wizard. They roughly swarm over his body and make sure he is truly dead.

"You saved my husband," Tala gushes, "and now we have saved you. It has been decades since we saw the Citadel of Ten Thousand Pearls. Would you like to see it with us?"

You nod slowly. You want to get out of Huzuz. Away from the Palace of the Enlightened Throne. Away from the dead sha'ir.

Turn to 66.

62

Honesty. It's really the only option, you decide. If you wander the grounds alone searching for the bottle, you could be caught and tossed into some dungeon for trespassing.

Besides, perhaps the Grand Caliph already has released the marid who is king of the Citadel of Ten Thousand Pearls. You could be searching for a djinni that is free. Perhaps the djinni already is electing to stay with the Grand Caliph, tired of his demanding wife, Tala. Your mind drifts along with the music until Gorar the barber finishes his performance.

He bows and snaps his fingers at you, indicating you should bring his barber kit. "I must practice my other skills on the Enlightened One," he whispers.

The pair of you move toward the massive chair in which the Grand Caliph sits. Closer to the man, you can tell that he is barely middle-aged. His flowing garments made him seem older and more imposing from a distance. The caliph grins at his barber friend. Imagine having so much power and wealth at his age!

"My friend, my beard is uneven. It is waiting for you to make it perfect."

"My caliph," the barber bows, then snaps his fingers at you.

You nervously rush up to the caliph's side, place the barber kit on the stone dais, and watch as the ruler's wives drift away into the garden. Now is the time, you decide.

"Y-Y-Y-Your Highness, Gr-Gr-Grand Caliph," you stutter.

You immediately note the surprise in the caliph's expression—surprise that an uninvited guest would address the ruler of the City of Delights. Still, he does not berate or silence you. He looks at you with curiosity.

Gorar the barber silently fumes at you.

"I am here on a grand mission," you continue, watching out the corner of your eye as a pair of guards strides closer. "I am here to rescue a sea djinni, the king of the Citadel of Ten Thousand Pearls. He might be trapped within your palace."

"Jamil! Stop your tales," Gorar scolds, grabbing his razor out of your hand and motioning you away. "I am sorry, O Caliph. My new friend is full of stories, it seems."

The caliph looks at you quizzically and stands. "Go on, young stranger."

The tale of your great adventure spills from your lips. By the time you are finished, you are winded, and the caliph has returned to his chair. He strokes his beard in contemplation.

"Jamil from Jumlat," he begins in measured tones. "Know you that I keep no djinn here against their wishes. Those who are in the palace are here because they are my friends. I do not believe in slavery. Still, I can tell by your honest voice that you truly believe what you say—that I have a bottle with a djinni trapped inside.

"If this is the case, I am saddened. No creature should be imprisoned unjustly. Therefore, young stranger, I shall take you to my room of bottles."

He stands again, and beckons you to join him. You watch the barber sigh and take a seat on the dais.

The Grand Caliph's course leads you through corridor after corridor of polished walnut and shining marble. No expense was spared in the creation of the buildings and courtyards within the palace walls. Eyeing the construction, you can tell newer buildings from old, evidence indeed that each caliph has worked to expand his holdings. Looking upward, you see a minaret that is being added on to. Perhaps it will dwarf the minarets of the Great Mosque near the Grand Bazaar.

Your attention snaps back to the Enlightened One.

You stop in a hallway of polished pink marble with black and gold veins. Floor, ceiling, and walls are made of the material, which is pleasing to the touch. The walls are decorated with sconces holding golden lamps filled with perfumed oil. The scent is musky and strong. Between the sconces, at precise, measured intervals, are paintings of handsome-looking men similar in appearance. These are likely paintings of caliph's relatives or ancestors, you muse.

The Grand Caliph opens a door of oak and steps inside. You follow quickly behind him. In the room play cases upon displays case filled with statues of griffins, hippogriffs, pegasi, and more. The most magnificent of the collection is a case of delicate glass griffins. All the statuary sparkles in the magical light of a glowing glass orb in the center of the ceiling. A tall, broad-shouldered guard stands in the far corner of the room. Beyond him is another door, similar to the one you just entered. He bows deeply to the Grand Caliph. The Enlightened One steps beyond him and stands in front of the next door.

The caliph turns and motions to you.

"This is your quest, young one. The room of bottles are beyond. Find the djinn of Fate!"

indeed he is here. And if he is not, you will leave this place quickly to search for this djinni elsewhere."

The caliph gestures toward the door. The guard looks on, his face an expressionless mask. Eager, you step forward.

Turn to 58.

63

The sha'ir is too late.

"Too late," you state simply. "The djinni is free. The bottle is broken."

"Then I shall break you, thief!" the sha'ir hisses. "If I cannot have the king of the Citadel of Ten Thousand Pearls, I will at least have my revenge."

He means to kill you!

You must do something!

You could run as far and as fast as your legs can take you. Perhaps you can lose him in the city beyond the palace. But, if you do, will you forever be on the run from him? Even so, it is better to run forever than die now.

On the other hand, have you come all this way to ? Have you bested a cyclops, a metal construct, and ntless no-count humans, assembled a magical car- rom fragments scattered throughout the Land of and freed two all-powerful djinn only to be stared by this upstart sorcerer?

u opt to flee, **turn to 59.**
 stand up and fight, **turn to 61.**

he glass griffins and pegasi, so delicate and form, is another door, similarly decorated. e guard, you open this door and step inside. eart leaps.

There are vases and bottles on shelves upon shelves upon shelves. Shelves that reach the ceiling nearly fifteen feet above the polished marble floor. There is no guard in this room. No doubt the guard in the room beyond serves that function.

You can see all the glassware perfectly, for a globe of magical light suspended from the mahogany ceiling above illuminates everything evenly.

Clear glass. Rose-colored glass. Glass the color of midnight. There are so many hues of glass, and in so many, many shapes. You try to take it all in and discover that it is difficult to guess how many pieces of glassware there are in this room.

"Hundreds," you whisper, selecting the bottom shelf to your right and inspecting as many bottles as you can at once. Some are sealed, some have loose-fitting tops. Some have no tops at all. A few have liquid inside, probably perfumes or fine liqueurs.

Your eyes blur from the numbers and colors and sizes and . . .

"There!" you exclaim.

A blue bottle on the bottom shelf. With other, thicker bottles in front of it, the fluted glass was nearly hidden. It looks for all of Zakhara like the twin of the bottle you found on the bottom of the Golden Gulf. You fall to your knees and gingerly extend your hand to clasp its neck. Carefully moving the other bottles from in front of it, you feel the smoothness of the glass. Odd, unlike the bottle at the bottom of the sea, you sense nothing about this one. No presence. Nothing urging you to open it.

Sitting cross-legged on the floor, you pull the bottle toward you and hold it with both hands. The seal is tight. You tug and tug and tug and fail to pull it free. "Hmmm," you think, "how to get this open?" You tug one last time, then set the bottle down in front of you and reach under your caftan for your pearling knife. It has stayed with you through all your adventures. The edge is still sharp, and you use it to pierce the bottle's seal, running the blade around the top until you feel it loosen in your hand. Replacing the knife, you tug on

the top again and fall backward when a billow of sea
foam escapes.

"Free!" shouts a spray of gray-green mist that erupts
from the bottle. "I'm free!" The mist dances and whirls,
twirls upward like a cyclone, and brightens to a dazzling
emerald green. "I . . . am . . . free!" The mist dances and
changes color again, this time to a brilliant blue.

The mist thickens and takes on a vaguely human
shape.

"Free!" the coalescing form of the sea djinni shouts in
an ear-splitting tone that rattles the shelves. "After all
these decades. FREE!" His booming voice shatters every
piece of glass in the room and causes you to crouch to
avoid the flying shards. Your action is useless, as you are
pelted by the pieces of glass, many chunks striking your
arms and face and drawing blood.

The guard rushes inside the room with his great
sword drawn, then retreats a step when he spies the
massive form of the djinni and the ruined glassware.

"Decades upon decades have I slept in that cursed
bottle, captured by my own foolishness!" The voice
fills the room, and you cup your hands over your ears
to deaden the noise. You notice the guard is doing likewise.

The djinni is massive and commanding. With rippling blue muscles and arms as thick as posts, he
stands in front of you, hands on his hips. You glance
upward into his angular face, and see his bright blue
eyes, the color of the Golden Gulf.

"Who has freed me?"

"J-J-Jamil," you answer, rising to your feet and carefully avoiding the glass all about you.

"My thanks, Jamil. You have ended an eternity of
torture. Away from my wife. Away from my city. Away
from all I held dear. My heart was as black as the bottom of the sea. Now to find my wife, Jamil. You must
help me! She is captive in a bottle like mine. An evil
sha'ir did this, a man who is expert at enslaving djinn.
That is why I need your help. A human would be
beneath his notice."

You try to interrupt him, but fail. The djinn rants on about how he and Tala were captured by the sha'ir in Sikak, City of Coins, and about how the sha'ir feared they would escape so he hid them away until he could grow more powerful. He seems oblivious to all but himself and has not even noticed you were cut by the flying glass.

The guard stares at the djinn in mute astonishment.

"The evil sha'ir fashioned a map, Jamil," the djinni's voice booms. "Out of a carpet."

"I know," you state simply, finally getting his attention. "On the carpet he embroidered a design that showed the location of the bottles containing you and Tala. Your wife is safe. She's somewhere outside of Sikak—waiting for me. She is waiting for you, too, hoping I would free you."

"And free me you did!" the djinni whoops. "And now I shall be reunited with my beloved. Again we will rule the Citadel of Ten Thousand Pearls!"

With that, the djinni's form dissolves into a spray of seafoam that thoroughly soaks you and the dumbfounded guard. The column of water shoots toward the ceiling and disappears.

"But what about my treasure?" you wail, looking at the broken glass all about you. "What about my dinars and pearls and my palace? I wanted to be a caliph."

"What about this mess?" the guard asks, finally finding his voice. "The caliph will want your head. You'll have to come with me."

The guard takes a step toward you and points with his sword to indicate you should walk in front of him.

"I've got other plans," you state, grinning sheepishly. With that, you sprint from the room, yipping when you step on a sharp piece of glass. The pain doesn't slow you, however. You know better than to let a palace guard drag you off to some dark dungeon.

You bolt beyond the broken griffins and pegasi. All of the beautiful glass animals were destroyed by the freed djinn's happiness.

Shattered beauty.

Outside you hear the pounding of footsteps. No doubt guards are on the way, drawn by the sound of breaking glass and the shouting djinni. And you know the guard from the glass rooms is on your heel. You slip into the shadows, confident you can sneak away from them all. But something sharp poking your back dashes your plans.

"Where is my djinni, Jamil?" The voice is coarse and low, but you recognize it.

The voice belongs to Sha'ir Rashad al-Azzazi.

"I tire of following you, young thief. I want my carpet. And I want the king of the Citadel of Ten Thousand Pearls."

You're too late, you think as you feel the sharp object, a knife no doubt, jab your back again.

"You will take me to the bottle."

Turn to 63.

65

Running appeals to you right now—despite the length of the construct's legs. You bound to your feet, grab all the sections of carpet, including the one the construct placed on you, and sprint toward the door. Risking a glance backward, you see the astonished construct open its mouth in surprise. You dash toward the darkened passageway that brought you here. In a half-dozen strides you are inside the comforting pitch darkness.

Slowing your pace, you run your elbow alongside the cavern wall so you can retrace your steps, ignoring the bumping and sharp corners of the stone. Remembering the path you took to get here, you picture the chamber with the flying eagles, and the larger chamber you fell into. Even though they will be dark, you should be able to navigate them well enough. Besides, once in a larger chamber, the carpet will whisk you away!

"By Haku!" you gasp as you emerge from the darkness into the treasure chamber. You could not have gotten yourself turned around in the corridor. Where is the cave with the eagle paintings? To make matters worse, standing right in front of you is the bronze construct.

"Little thief," the guardian booms. "You were foolish to steal from my master—even if it was such a trivial thing as a rug."

"Your master's dead!" you protest as he grabs you about the waist and picks you up until you are eye-to-eye with him. The carpet sections fall from your grasp.

"Put me down!" you demand.

"You should not have taken what belonged to the sha'ir," the giant drones. "My orders are clear."

You feel his fists tighten about your waist, and the wind rushes from your lungs. He slowly squeezes until the last breath of life flees from you, and your body falls limp to join the coins and the carpet on the floor.

THE END

66

The colors of the palace melt and whirl, making you dizzy and anxious. You cannot see the forms of the two djinn at your side, but you sense they are with you on this fantastic journey. For a seeming eternity the colors collide, then they separate and turn a muted blue as you feel cool water close about your skin. For an instant you panic, fearing you will drown. But then you realize you are breathing the water as if you were a fish born to it.

Sea djinn swim before you. Following the king and queen, you angle your body down toward what looks like the sea floor.

Your mind reels as you take in the Citadel. More than a building, it is a city—as large as Huzuz and

Jumlat put together. Spires, domes, and towers stretch to the waves above. The buildings are massive; their many levels are tall enough to accommodate the forms of twenty-foot djinn. The buildings sparkle warmly. They are made out of pearls!

You spend the day in the city, meeting the powerful blue and green djinn who live there. You forget all about your dreams of wealth, realizing that helping the king and queen was an adventure worth more than the tallest pile of gold dinars.

When your visit is over, the king closes his massive hand about your wrist, nods to his wife Tala, then he rises from the ocean floor with you in tow. You shoot from the waves and into the air like a sailfish. The warm air plays across your skin, drying and refreshing you.

The king grins at you. "Return to visit whenever you desire, Jamil. We will always open our home to you, and you will always be able to find it. Just think of Tala and me."

His course takes the pair of you far across the Golden Gulf until you spy the familiar sights of your home in the distance. Going home. The thought makes you happy. Still, you've had a wonderful adventure. One that you will remember for all of your days.

You near the shore and the king deposits you on a familiar dock. The sailors and rope boys gape in astonishment.

The king pats you on the back, waves farewell, and jets into the sky, his blue form quickly melding with the colors above and disappearing from view.

You are still in the caftan provided by your mischievous Huzuz guide. But it is in perfect condition, showing no signs of your battle with the evil sha'ir.

Essaf the Hungry is there on the docks, too, as are the rest of the divers from his ship.

It is dawn in the City of Multitudes.

"Snap to, Jamil!" the Hungry One bellows as if nothing has happened over the past many days. "You are late, and it is time to shove off! If you are late again, I'll demote you to rope boy!" Essaf jumps onto his boat, and you see the gazes of your fellow pearl divers fix on you.

You are not the same person who dived from Essaf's boat several days ago. Perhaps your friends sense that. You have changed. You take a step forward to join your old friends, and you feel something heavy inside the pocket of your caftan.

You thrust your hand inside, and your fingers close around a handful of fat pearls. Bringing them out into the dawn sky, your face breaks into a broad grin. They are priceless fat black pearls—a gift from the King and Queen of the Citadel of Ten Thousand Pearls! You are rich after all!

You look at Essaf's boat, tuck the pearls back into your pocket, then glance up and down the wharf.

"I quit, Essaf. But you've not seen the last of me. Perhaps we'll run into each other on the Golden Gulf—where my divers and rope boys will beat you to the best pearls."

There are ships for sale on the docks, you are certain. With the wealth in your pocket you can buy the one of your choice—and pay for rope boys and divers of your own.

Waving farewell to your friends, you stride away from a surprised Essaf. After you pick out a ship, you will visit the marketplace and shop until you are tired. Tomorrow you will hire a crew.

The sun inches out over Jumlat's mirrorlike bay. Its first rays make the water sparkle golden. The breeze dances gently across your skin as you pick up your pace.

Today is a wondrous day indeed!

THE END